M000074098

The Beauty of Their Youth

American Storytellers

Philip Baruth
American Zombie Beauty

Joyce Hinnefeld
The Beauty of Their Youth

The Beauty of Their Youth

Stories

Joyce Hinnefeld

Wolfson Press

The author is grateful to the editors of the following publications where these stories first appeared:

Center: A Journal of the Literary Arts, "Everglades City."

Arts & Letters: A Journal of Contemporary Culture, "A Better Law of Gravity."

The Literary Review, "Benedicta, Or a Guide to the Artist's Resumé."

Referential, "Polymorphous."

Cover design by Sky Santiago

Copyright © 2020 by The Trustees of Indiana University
All rights reserved. First edition.

ISBN: 9781950066049

Wolfson Press
Master of Liberal Studies Program
Indiana University South Bend
1700 Mishawaka Avenue
South Bend, Indiana, 46634-7111
WolfsonPress.com

Contents

Series Introduction and Preface

THE AMERICAN STORYTELLERS SERIES AT WOLFSON PRESS promotes genres of writing that have been neglected by major publishing houses. We join several other small presses in seeking to provide a quality publishing outlet for books of shorter fiction and nonfiction, such as the short story, the novella, the short memoir, and the literary essay. Few commercial publishers today acknowledge a market for these forms. We believe, however, that much of the best American writing falls outside the scope of the novel and the book-length work of nonfiction. A flourishing mastery of the shorter genres is supported by a literary magazine culture and by longstanding practices in graduate education. Most fiction writers, for example, begin their careers as short story writers. For these writers a fine short fiction piece is often not the first step in the development of a novel, but a complete artistic statement. Shorter works, whether in essay or story form, can coalesce into powerful collections that express a sharp creative vision peculiar to the form. We hope to bring rich collections of this kind to our ambitious readers by showcasing the best short works by new and established writers.

The writers in this series entertain us and relieve us of our personal burdens, only to trouble us with experiences and ways of thinking that collide with our normal assumptions. Shorter forms are particularly well suited to play this disruptive role in our imaginations and to spur us to flashes of daring reflection, because they soon leave us on our own again. They don't promise to take care of us for very long. What short stories or essays set up, in the way a novel can't, is a series of encounters or collisions that require quick adjustments — more like dating than marriage. Who's to say what these intimate experiences may prepare us for?

Taken together, the five short stories in Joyce Hinnefeld's collection *The Beauty of Their Youth* explore a deep problem of time and memory. Hinnefeld demonstrates that time isn't really a stream that carries us always into the future, without return. Instead, the past remains to be lived. Human memory complicates the natural flow of Newtonian time, creating eddies and counter-flowing streamlets that take us back to a past that can still surprise us and change us. The characters attempt to seize life and to control, name, and own their fates, even as another truth, alien to their intentions, is emerging.

The problem is most fully revealed in the title story of the collection. Fran, a middle-aged woman who takes her college-aged daughter to Greece and Italy to revisit the places and people she knows from her student exchange experience, gradually discovers what that phase of her past life really meant to her friends. Only now, much later, does she learn what happened then. The stories present us with an almost Proustian understanding of time. For Fran, it isn't merely a matter of being confronted with or uncovering unsuspected facts; she comes to see that she was not the person that she long believed she was.

In the other stories in this volume, we encounter characters who are surprised to realize that the most intimate or apparently obvious and unremarkable facts of their existence contain mysteries. This insight has the force of truth. It happens ineluctably. In our minds, ordinary objects (like the dusty blue, dried-up washcloth in "A Better Theory of Gravity") crystalize into symbols over time. If (like the German tourist Inge in "Everglades City") we allow ourselves the freedom to follow our whims and desires, believing that we are expressing our personal truth, we discover with a fateful clarity that our lives are empty of meaning. And the people who seem most familiar to us may turn out to have survived largely as fantasies in the stories we've told ourselves; as in "Polymorphous," they can appear to step out of themselves suddenly into another, unsuspected identity.

These are stories of awakening, but not in the "rite of passage" sense so familiar to us in the world of American fiction. Here we awaken from the dream of the life we've been living purposefully for a long time. These stories give a pointed precision to an insight that haunts Joyce Hinnefeld's fine novels, namely, that mistaken perceptions and misguided decisions, rather than tragic flaws that must destroy us, are inextricably part of the ordinary texture of our lives. Our flaws, not foreign or ultimately even "wrong," are intimately at home among the characteristic peculiarities that define our humanity. This is a vision that understands without excusing, joining the past self to the future self, and one person to another, in a community in which we share responsibility for the stories that we tell.

Joseph Chaney, Series Editor
American Storytellers

For Gene Garber

Polymorphous

BY THE TIME SHE WAS 20, WITH A LITTLE BABY AND A HOUSEHOLD to run, Joan had already started to seem like some sort of local exotic to her friends from high school, home from college on their breaks. All because she canned her own vegetables and sewed her own clothes and breastfed her son, at a time and in a place where those things wouldn't come back into fashion for a good while. Now, forty years later, she still gardened and canned and sewed. She'd even gone back to school and finished her own degree eventually, with a nice and useless and exotic major in English. But by now the thing that made her colorful in the eyes of her friends and neighbors was her weekly outing with her eighty-year-old neighbor, a gay man named Richard Meredith.

Richard and his partner Bobby had been among the earliest of the weekenders from New York to arrive in their corner of Bucks County, Pennsylvania back in the sixties, when Joan was a teenager. Now the whole region was dotted with tastefully remodeled stone farmhouses and lavish gardens, weekend homes for people from New York and Philadelphia, many of them, in the preferred idiom of the older locals, "boys" and "girls"— which seemed to be an easier way to speak of it than the more distasteful "gays" or "lesbians." People who just hadn't quite grown up yet, but never mind, that was all right. They were good neighbors; they took good care of their places and kept the local economy humming along. No one wanted to stir up trouble by being offended.

By this summer—the summer of 2010, when Joan would turn sixty—Bobby had been dead for twenty years. Today was Joan's day to take Richard for groceries and their usual stop at the library. Richard had never learned to drive, and for nineteen of the years since Bobby's death it had been Joan's mother Elsa who drove him to town each week. She'd done it until a year ago, until the week before she died. And now it was Joan's job, though she couldn't say exactly why.

She'd tried to make the best of it. After the supermarket and the library they might go to one of the restaurants on Main Street, to one of the places Richard liked because the waiters were young and handsome and doted on him. And Joan didn't mind, because the food was generally good if ridiculously overpriced, the coffee strong and hot, the way she'd make it at home.

At a little after ten she strapped on her seatbelt and started the engine of her old Dodge. The truth was she was settling into the role of local eccentric—the quiet reader; the shunner of modern conveniences; the woman who, even though her kids had grown up and moved on, was only minimally involved in her church; the luncher with one of the old New York boys— finally deciding, at nearly sixty, that it suited it her. All right then, she thought as she turned around in the driveway and headed down the gravel lane: time to embrace this person she'd become. Once again she'd be Richard's chauffeur and, mostly, his audience, as he generally did most of the talking. All right. So be it.

Today would surely be different though. Just three days ago she'd driven an irritable and impatient Richard home from the hospital, where'd he'd spent two days and a night undergoing a battery of tests, all of which had come back negative. "I'm as healthy as I've ever been, as I kept trying to tell them," he complained as Joan drove him home. "If they'd only been willing to listen to me, they might have saved us all a great deal of time and money and maddening inconvenience. But of course it's the insurance money they're after, as we all bloody well know." Joan said nothing; it seemed better just to let him rant, though she wondered if it was good for him, going on that way.

He'd had a dizzy spell. "Just stood up too quickly from weeding the garden," he said. His niece, visiting from Long Island for the day ("She's had her eye on my antiques since she was a teenager," Richard had told Joan the week before, when the niece called to say she wanted to visit him), had been watching him from his kitchen window. She saw him wobble as he stood up, reaching for the cottage wall to steady himself, and insisted on driving him to the emergency room.

"I only agreed to go to get away from her," he said as Joan drove him home from the hospital. Today, three days later, Joan had called to suggest that he just give her his shopping list and a list of books he wanted from the library. No need for him to make the trip into town that week, she said.

But "Don't be silly," he'd told her. "I'm *fine*. I'll look for you at ten, as usual." And he'd hung up the phone.

Now, as Joan drove down the lane, a rock pinged her windshield and she winced, then relaxed, reminding herself that they could, in fact, afford a new windshield, or even a new car, if they truly needed one. The farm, or what was left of it, was theirs outright, and for years her husband Glen, a skilled carpenter, had had more work than he wanted or needed with all the avid remodelers who'd moved in around them. Now he had the luxury of turning down jobs when people called, but, still healthy and strong and happiest when he was in his shop, he rarely did. Joan pulled off their lane onto the county road, wondering idly why she found it so hard to relax and accept this newfound ease.

Probably it was partly worry about Pam, her daughter, divorced and with two teenage sons to support. But even Pam was doing better now, working for her brother—the successful bachelor—in New York. A beast of a commute, all by bus, but she was up to it, Pam said. *So there*, Joan said to Elsa in her mind. Her mother had had opinions about Joan and Glen's parenting style, ones she didn't keep to herself. Too permissive; what would become of them, how would they ever learn to be responsible? *But look: they're fine.* Pam's boys too, mostly.

It was a pleasant morning, cool for June, and a month shy of a year since Elsa's death. It had been a wet, cold spring so far this year, but the summer before there'd been a terrible drought, the second in three years, and though her mother's death, on the Fourth of July, had been unexpected, in hindsight Joan wondered if Elsa hadn't just decided she couldn't face another parched and miserable summer; she'd hated the heat.

She'd especially hated the heat there on the farm—watching the corn and beans in the surrounding fields turn shriveled and brown, the creek bed dry as dust. But then who didn't hate a drought? Elsa hated the winter too, because nothing grew then, and more often than not everything was coated with a thick layer of dirty ice. She could complain about any season. In the summer, the weeds and the poison ivy were going to be the death of her yet. The truth was, Joan knew, she just hated the farm.

Her heart simply gave out, the paramedics had said. It was Richard who'd found her, lying at the end of her bedraggled delphiniums, while Joan and Glen drove home from a barbecue with Pam and the boys. And Joan hadn't been able to decide whether she'd failed her mother by being gone that day or had, in fact, given her a kind of gift.

A mist rose off her neighbor's cornfield as she drove the hundred yards to Richard's drive, and there was a hint of hazy sunlight. It was the kind of day that could go either way. Up ahead she saw that Richard had walked down the short lane from his tidy, ivy-covered house, which, when Joan's grandfather owned three times the acreage she and Glen now owned and oversaw a thriving Pennsylvania Dutch farm, had been a sharecropper's cottage.

He stood next to the mailbox, leaning on his cane. Joan bristled at this affectation—her first reaction, but then she caught herself. What if Richard really was sick, what if there was something seriously wrong? He'd always seemed to her as strong as an ox, stubborn and bull-headed as some large animal too. She'd seen him age, of course, but it was hard for her to imagine him as sick or frail. Earlier that week, in fact the day his niece arrived, she'd looked out the kitchen window to see him bushwhacking his way up the overgrown path from the creek, where he'd gone to pick the jewelweed he liked to keep in a vase on his windowsill.

Now his old black sweater was buttoned to the neck, and he wore a jaunty black beret. He was, Joan assumed, trying to look like a contented country gentleman—French provincial maybe— idling there by his freshly painted mailbox on this damp and misty morning. But Joan recognized the impatience in the way he was gripping his cane. She was fifteen minutes late, and as he strolled across the narrow road to the passenger side of her car, she tried to decide whether to apologize.

"Ah, the slow, drowsy mornings of we happy retirees," he said after he'd slammed the door and struggled into his seatbelt. "I trust you were lingering over a good cup of coffee and our illustrious local newspaper. Maybe you were as fascinated as I was by the contentious debate at last night's Sewage Board meeting?"

The usual trace of an accent—something like Richard's notion of England by way of Boston, the voice of someone like Henry James; this was what Joan always assumed he had in mind—set her teeth on edge. She rolled her window halfway down and sniffed the wet, green air, knowing the draft would bother him but for the moment not caring. "I'm not sure what it is you think I'm 'retired' from," she said as she put the car in gear and continued driving. "And good morning to you too, Richard."

As she drove she glanced over at him and wondered if he wasn't a little paler than usual. When he coughed she rolled her window up and said, "You know, I wish you'd just let me get your groceries this week. You probably ought to stay home and rest."

He shook his head and cleared his throat. "I've told you, Joan, I'm fine." He unbuttoned several buttons of his sweater and glanced at her, then turned his head to gaze out his own window. "It's just that it's a little damp out today." He paused, for only a beat. "And of course I had to wait quite a while for you to arrive."

She smiled to herself, hearing that. But she didn't apologize.

At the supermarket they went their separate ways as always, Richard steering his basket toward the deli counter, Joan lingering in the produce section. Later, Richard found her at the dairy case and helped her reach a carton of heavy cream far to the back of the high top shelf. At moments like this, Joan felt distinctly uncomfortable. Despite the difference in their ages, despite Richard's clearly aging body, she felt small and weak when she saw herself through his eyes. And also rather dowdy. Normally she was fond of her long braid of reddish hair with its many strands of gray (another eccentricity: she chose not to dye her hair), her open face with its laugh lines and wrinkles from years spent working outdoors. But whenever she went anywhere with Richard, she wondered why she didn't try to fix herself up more—put on make-up, dress in nice slacks and heels, like other women her age, instead of jeans and sneakers.

She felt it powerfully this morning, again, this time when Richard suddenly turned into the pharmacy section as she stood searching among the endless pink and purple boxes for a simple box of Kotex pads. She stood there as he wheeled his cart towards her, staring silently at him, suddenly remembering how she'd felt when Richard and Bobby had first started renting the cottage, back when she'd been a lonely, painfully shy girl, humiliated by recent changes in her own body, awash in questions she'd had no one to ask. She knew better than to pose them to her distant, bitter mother, whose answer to all her daughter's dreams and yearnings would have been to tell her to go to church. Even though she herself hadn't been to church in years.

Odd to think of all that now—the way she used to feel around Richard and Bobby, like they knew so much more than she'd ever understand, like they could see everything about her. Bobby, in particular, had made her feel that way. She was tormented by how beautiful he was, back in those early years—his dark curls and long, dark lashes, his brilliant smile, his lean, olive-skinned body. She'd created elaborate fantasies around him, ones where he kissed her, ones where he led her deep in the woods and held her hard against a tree and then made love to her on a bed of pine needles. Alone in her room late on a Friday night, she would watch Richard and Bobby arriving at the cottage and unpacking whatever old car they'd borrowed to drive there; through her window she could just make out their separate outlines, pulling boxes and bags out of the trunk, in the dim light from the bulb next to the cottage's back door. She always thought she might see them kiss or embrace, but she never did. And so she let herself imagine that in fact Bobby was waiting for her, waiting until she was a little bit older, when he would reach for her hand one day along the creek, and take her into the woods.

Now, wheeling his cart towards her, Richard seemed to take her silent staring as embarrassment at being caught in the feminine hygiene aisle. "Don't worry, dear," he deadpanned as he passed her cart, patting her arm. "We do know that such things happen, and we sympathize."

You don't know the half of it, she'd wanted to say. She wished she had the courage to tell him that that particular embarrassing thing hadn't happened to her for a while now. What she needed the pads for were increasingly frequent issues with bladder control. Little trickles of pee in her underwear. Oh, the perils of growing older, she might say to him. Would he find that funny? But it was Richard who made jokes about people's bodies, she thought, not her. So she only nodded and gave a half-hearted laugh as he rolled on past her.

He could be charming, and wickedly funny. But she hated to admit that for some reason. She wasn't sure why. It was certainly true, though, that in the year since her mother's death, when Joan had taken over the job of checking in with Richard and driving him into town each week, he'd begun to annoy her even more. Her mother hadn't minded Richard at all, it seemed; in fact, she'd seemed to relish his jokes about the neighbors, his pleasure in local gossip about train-wreck marriages and teenage pregnancies and drunk-driving arrests. She'd had too much contempt for her neighbors to gossip about them herself, but her mother would always listen to Richard—at the fence between their gardens, or over a cup of coffee at her kitchen table—a small smile playing at the corners of her mouth. Remarkable really, in a woman who hardly ever smiled.

In the years after he and Bobby first arrived, Joan had mostly felt free to ignore Richard. He'd been only a peripheral part of her life for most of the years he'd been her neighbor. Bobby, of course, was another story. When they first rented the cottage, in 1965, Bobby was twenty-five and by far the friendlier of the two. Richard had claimed to be the same age, and it was only after Bobby's death that Joan realized he'd been lying, that he was, in fact, at least fifteen years older than Bobby. Back in those days, you really couldn't tell. Richard was strong and vital; he'd looked far younger than he was. Not that Joan was looking at him much.

Soon after they rented the white-washed stone cottage Richard had set his sights on making it into a weekend showplace for their friends from the city. Within a few years its western wall was dense with well-trained English ivy that bordered the brick chimney, and the surrounding gardens were filled with delicate lily-of-the-valley and fiddlehead ferns in the spring, then Asian lilies and towering cosmos and giant yellow dahlias grown from bulbs that were an early gift from Elsa. She'd been unnaturally fond of Richard from the beginning, it seemed to Joan. Only later would it dawn on her that her mother and Richard were nearly the same age.

Maybe it was because Elsa and all the other neighbors called them "the boys," but that was exactly how Joan remembered Richard and Bobby from those early years—as exuberant, youthful boys with brash and colorful friends. She remembered watching from her bedroom window on a snowy night just before Christmas as a whole crew of them arrived, well after midnight, rolling out of someone's rusted old Cadillac and sliding giddily down the slope behind the barn to the ice-covered creek below. They often came with big groups in the summer, too, and then she'd hear them splashing and yelling in the creek. Further along in the woods was a place where the creek narrowed, then opened out to form a deeper pool, a place where, in the early summer after a spring with lots of rain, a person could actually swim. This, Richard had told her recently, had been dubbed "the pool of desire" by one of their friends.

When Bobby died no one had called it AIDS, though it clearly was. Richard never talked about Bobby's illness or his death, but his grief was obvious. The most vivid sign of it was the fact that when he returned to the cottage the following spring, after an absence of several months (Bobby had died, they later learned, slowly and painfully, in a hospital in New York), and informed Elsa that he would now be living in the cottage full-time, Richard no longer looked, in any way, like a boy. Instead he looked like what, in truth, he was: a sixty-year-old man, bereft, robbed of his one great love. He was heavier then, and his thinning hair, now cropped close, had gone completely gray. He immersed himself in his gardens, and though a few friends still visited from time to time, he spent most of his days alone.

When they finished their shopping and some browsing at the library, Richard insisted on taking Joan out to lunch at a new place that he wanted to try. While they waited for their salads they talked about the books they'd checked out. Richard had a new book on Frank Lloyd Wright, one on English gardens, and one on interior design inspired by the Bauhaus group, artists he proceeded to tell Joan about in exhaustive detail, paying no attention to her glazed expression or the impatient tapping of her foot below the table. He liked to dwell on books like these, she often thought, to punish her, because he knew she had little interest in things having to do with art and design. Or certainly no particular skill or understanding when it came to such things. What she cared about was making sure things worked (the car, the chimneys, the septic system), and having plenty of good food to eat. She was a vegetable grower, not a gardener; she'd kept Elsa's beds pruned and weeded, to the extent that she had, out of some sort of loyalty to her mother, not any particular interest in flowers.

When at last Richard's pasta arrived and he paused to take some eager bites, Joan started by telling him about the Margaret Atwood novel she'd checked out, an older one that someone in her book group had told her about, and then the collection of short stories by an Irish author named William Trevor. This one had been suggested by her friend Reeva, who'd been another "nontraditional student" in the evening college where Joan had finished her degree, slowly making her way through all the required courses, beginning back when her daughter started school. It was from a story in this collection that Reeva had learned the term "poofter." Now when she called, after they'd exchanged news about their children and grandchildren, Reeva would sometimes ask, "And how's the old poofter next door?" And then they'd both chuckle a little guiltily.

Now, for some reason, Joan felt like telling Richard about this. "You know," she said as she buttered a slice of thick brown bread from the basket between them, "in Ireland they apparently refer to men like you as 'poofters'. At least that's the term this William Trevor uses in one of his stories."

She coughed a bit then, choking on the piece of bread she'd stuffed in her mouth as soon as she'd made this studiedly offhand remark. She couldn't quite believe she'd said it. They rarely went anywhere near the subject of Richard's sexual orientation, or anything else as personal as that, during their lunchtime conversations. Not because Joan wasn't curious. In fact she was intensely curious, and had been since she was a girl. There'd been all kinds of people back there in the "pool of desire," she knew, at various times: men and women both, all ages, different races. Were the women always with the women then, and the men with the men? Bobby—trim, dark, boylike and movie star-handsome Bobby—too?

Richard stared at her, then blinked and looked down at his plate as he speared an oily sun-dried tomato. He held it near his lips for a moment, just long enough to reply, "Well, yes, I've heard that term. And here's one for you, a name men like me use for people like you, at our less charitable moments: we sometimes call you 'breeders'." With that he bit into the slippery tomato with relish and smiled at her. He chewed it two or three times, then added, "Rather like cows, you understand."

His bluntness shocked her; he could take her breath away at times. But he also made her laugh—probably more than anyone she knew.

She laughed now, gratefully. "'Breeders'," she said as she dipped into her soup. "That's good. Reeva will appreciate that one."

And it was good. Certainly better than a word like "poofter," which sounded like something a seven-year-old on a playground might have come up with. "Breeders," on the other hand, was clever. Clever, and a little vicious, like Richard and his friends.

And like Elsa, who might well have referred to her daughter as a breeder. Or as a cat in heat. She *did* call Joan that once, one memorable evening when she'd found a condom in the upstairs toilet, one that Glen thought he'd managed to flush away. Bitter as Elsa was about so much—an unwanted life of trying to run a farm, a husband who drank and left her not long after their daughter was born, neighbors whose sympathy only made her angrier—never, it seemed, did she direct any of her bitterness at her son-in-law or grandchildren. Or her happy-go-lucky boy tenants. Perhaps it was because of all the work Richard had done for her through the years, before Joan married Glen—though he'd bartered mightily with that work. One summer, before he and Bobby had saved enough to buy the cottage from Elsa and were still renting, he'd rebuilt the stone wall surrounding the farmhouse and barn; the next he'd repaired the barn's leaking roof. Both times, Elsa had given up half a year's rent in exchange. Richard became, in a sense, her mother's right-hand man, until Joan married Glen. Odd as it was to think such a thing, in certain ways Richard had been like a husband to Elsa.

Thinking of that, Joan always came back to the same memory—of her mother's death, of the whole series of strange, unfocused moments that day. What should have been a horror somehow hadn't been, thanks to Richard. They'd gotten the call late in the afternoon and driven home immediately. At the end of their lane, they'd found an ambulance in the driveway. When Joan hurried from the car toward the front door of the barn, she'd heard Richard call her name.

He was sitting in a lawn chair by one of Elsa's flower beds, beside her prone body. Behind him the paramedics stood at a respectful distance, waiting. He had straightened Elsa's legs and smoothed her house dress, folded her hands at her waist, called the ambulance. Joan could picture Richard fussing over Elsa's fallen body, the same way he methodically pruned and weeded his flower beds and swept his front porch every morning. He had closed Elsa's eyes and tidied her hair. He had handled everything.

At lunch that day she thought of asking Richard about this. How is it that you thought to make my mother look presentable before they came for her, before Glen and I saw her? How is it that you're a man and I'm a woman, and you found something when she died—something like beauty—that I never saw in her?

By the time they drove home the day had turned sunny and warm. Even Richard seemed to be welcoming the sun with a kind of relaxed expansiveness. Joan could see that he was tired, yet he had left his sweater unbuttoned, his beret in his lap, and he'd unrolled his window a good two inches. They rode in silence for the first half of the drive.

But Joan was stuck on the past, on Bobby, on all those people swimming in the deep pool in the woods. She roused herself and glanced over at Richard. "So what kinds of things went on back there?" she asked suddenly, out of the blue, knowing he wouldn't give her a straightforward answer. "Back there in the creek?"

He cleared his throat and sniffed. "Are you asking whether animals were also involved?"

She shook her head and laughed. "All right then," she said. "Never mind."

He sighed and gazed through the windshield. "Well of course there was a little of everything," he said. "Breeders with breeders and poofters with poofters and sometimes breeders with poofters. The whole happy lot." He looked over at her. "Surely you read some Freud in one or another of that endless string of college classes you took, Joan. As the great man said, we're all polymorphous perverts at heart. Male, female, why all the categories and barriers? There's room for a little of everything."

She nodded as she slowed the car and turned on her signal for the approach to Richard's cottage. She tried to imagine how Elsa might have felt about that, and about the goings-on in the creek on her property on those weekends years ago. She had to have known about it.

"I wonder what my mother would have thought about all that," she said, anticipating his biting response.

But when he answered he wasn't smiling, or laughing. "I'm not sure. If you wanted to know, you should have asked her," he said. They had stopped in front of the cottage, and he rolled up his window and turned to her before he opened his door, adding, "She always seemed to enjoy herself, on the occasions when she joined us." Then he winked at her and heaved himself out of the car, leaning heavily on his cane.

She turned off the engine and scrambled out of the car to help him with his groceries, shaking her head and laughing again, but more tentatively. "Right," she said. "I can just imagine Elsa joining in on something like that." Straight face or not, he was surely joking, she thought. Wasn't he? But he was already several steps ahead of her, pulling a bag from the back seat and walking over to unlock the door.

Once inside the tidy little kitchen, Joan bustled around him, trying to help him put things away, getting in his way and getting on his nerves, she could tell. Why didn't she just bring him a little supper later on? she said. But no, he said; he was looking forward to broiling the fish he'd bought. But first he wanted to stretch out on the chaise lounge in the garden for a while. He picked up one of his library books and shooed her toward the door.

She turned to him once more before he could close the door behind her. "You were kidding when you said that, right?" she said. "About Elsa enjoying herself back there in the creek?"

"Well, as I said, Joan, you should have asked her about that. She'd have told you, I suppose. If you'd asked."

He looked exhausted, Joan realized, as he closed the door. That's what had happened to her mother too. Some dizzy spells, exhaustion—and a few weeks later she was dead.

After she put her own groceries away, Joan pulled on her old rubber boots and tramped along the creek, back into the woods, to the deepest part. The pool of desire.

It was so full and rich for June, so different from the summer before. She roused a couple dragonflies as she approached, and she looked down at what had to be hundreds of minnows, darting in every direction, senselessly. Driven by their own desires.

Yes, she'd read or heard that phrase from Freud, "polymorphous perverts," in some class at some point. She remembered that the "perverts" part had bothered her.

Now she stared at the creek, rushing over the rocks before settling into the clear, still pool. She thought of other afternoons years ago—ripping off her shorts and t-shirt, her bra and underpants, then clutching at Glen as he held her in the deep water—and a shiver of pleasure ran through her. She turned in the direction of the cottage, catching a glimpse of one white wall and the top of the chimney through the trees. She imagined Richard in his garden in back, alone, seated amongst his lilies, reading about beautiful things. And she wondered what she would do without him.

A Better Law of Gravity

[The old Frankie] agreed with Berenice about the main laws of her creation, but she added many things: an aeroplane and a motorcycle to each person, a world club with certificates and badges, and a better law of gravity.

Carson McCullers, *The Member of the Wedding*

IT WAS THE SUMMER AFTER HER FIRST YEAR OF COLLEGE, AND FJ, who no longer wished to be called Frankie, was listless and blue. College had been disappointing, and home was worse. But then one morning things turned interesting.

It began, that crazy green August morning, with a scene FJ viewed through the windshield of a car: Janice from the neck down, running to catch up with a woman in tight blue jeans, whose shoulders, neck and head were outside the frame of FJ's vision. Must be someone Janice knows from work or something, FJ thought, not quite taking it in when instead of catching up to the blue-jeaned woman and tapping her on the shoulder or calling out hello or some such thing, Janice suddenly reared up and kicked the woman in her shapely, gently swaying behind.

"Boyoman," FJ whispered to herself as she sank down in the passenger seat, alarmed but curious and wondering what her sister-in-law might do next.

The shapely woman turned around and stood there, apparently speechless, while Janice's body, now running back toward the car, filled the frame of the windshield.

"That'll teach that bitch to steal my blue jeans and flaunt her fat old ass in front of my husband!" she hissed into FJ's ear, and then she squealed into reverse.

It was a Firebird she drove, only a few years old. Jarvis's new car. "Mark my words, he'll notice it's gone well before he notices I'm gone," Janice said that morning, twitching in neutral outside the little suburban house.

Aunt Pet was in the kitchen cutting up a chicken when FJ woke to the sound of the engine and walked outside. She was still in her gym shorts and ratty old T-shirt, sleep caked in the corners of her eyes, and she approached the Firebird tentatively, wondering who could be inside.

"Get in, squirt," Janice said, "before the old battle-axe figures out who's out here."

And FJ had two thoughts in quick succession then. The first was that this must be what they meant about what happened when Janice didn't take her medication. The second was just a fleeting picture, one that came to her from time to time that summer for no apparent reason: her roommate's dried-up washcloth hanging on the rack on the back of the door of their freshman dorm room the preceding year. She climbed, barefoot and already sweating at nine in the morning, into the passenger seat of Jarvis's new-to-him Firebird. And then they were gone.

"Just a blip on the screen, too fast for their old pansy-ass radar," Janice was saying, whipping around a curve. She punched in the cigarette lighter and rummaged in her bag. "Here," she said and handed the bag to FJ. "Get out my cigarettes. And help yourself."

She will never call me Frankie, FJ thought. She doesn't even know who I am right now.

FJ didn't expect to go anywhere near Janice and Jarvis's hometown, thirty miles from her own home in central Georgia, which she shared with her father and her aunt. But then there they were, long enough to kick that woman's ass. In and out in a hurry though, right onto the highway after that, speeding along like a couple of banshees and Janice, at least, was clearly giving the finger to the world. What FJ was doing was unclear, even to her.

"Janice, that woman stole your blue jeans?"

"Well, theft is theft, isn't it? I mean, yes, I believe she did, that is she showed up downtown wearing the exact same pair I have and then she walked around town bouncing that big high-rise butt all day long. So yes, she did steal the idea of those particular blue jeans from me. For my husband's benefit."

"Jarvis knows her?"

"He'll claim he doesn't. He'll claim a lot of things, believe you me, little girl."

While watching a companion kick a near stranger on the street might have struck some people as alarming, what FJ felt was that Janice's reaction to this woman was interesting but perhaps not that out of the ordinary. FJ was not yet all that experienced in the ways of love, or the ways of men and women and other women and all that that entailed. And the truth was, she didn't really know her sister-in-law. For years she hardly ever saw her. And when she did there was that horrible embarrassment from the past to contend with, the wedding day, her awful adolescent longing and desperate pleading and well, suffice it to say that she preferred not to see her brother and sister-in-law at all for quite some time afterwards, and when she did, they said very little to each other.

Was it maturity on her part, that is the ability to see things more clearly, she wondered, or did Janice look more desperate than desirable these days? Hadn't she aged more than she should have since her wedding six years before? She'd grown bony and dark under the eyes and become a chain smoker with a harsh, hacking cough. "Jarvis says sometimes she forgets to take the medication and then they've got some trouble on their hands," Aunt Pet said one night after dinner, to which FJ's father had replied in his customary way, leaving the table and sitting down with his newspaper.

Still, despite a lingering sense that her father and her aunt had the idea something was wrong, FJ might have gone on seeing all of this as a side to Janice she'd simply had no reason to know about. Except for the conversation when they stopped later that morning for breakfast.

They were in a diner in a town that FJ didn't know, and when she pulled her dusty bare feet up to hide them under her suntanned legs on the vinyl seat of their corner booth, she felt glad the place was filled with strangers.

It seemed like everyone, not just Janice, was smoking; the blinds were pulled against the white hot morning sun, and the smell of coffee and cigarettes and the buzz of conversation surrounded them in a pleasant, muffling cloud. The waitress brought tall glasses of water and filled the coffee cup that Janice had turned over before she'd even slid into her seat. FJ opened her menu and started to relax, thinking to herself that maybe she and her sister-in-law would start doing this more often, just head out on a Saturday morning every now and then for a nice drive and breakfast in a new town.

Maybe they'd finally get to know each other a little better. FJ relished the idea of having this woman—the woman she'd so adored and dreamed of when she was a sad and troublesome child—as a friend. Maybe even a close one. But then they started talking.

What FJ said was "Well, it's been some time since we've seen each other, Janice."

And what Janice said went something like this: "Yes, yes, the little girl is gone and grown and aren't we all glad of that? And well you thought it'd all come out different in the end and so did I but then the end has yet to come. And all of this"—she waved her hands around her face, the restaurant booth—"is all the same whatever time it is. We're coming loose is all. We're coming loose." And she laughed and lit another cigarette, nearly dropping it, lit, in her purse when something else occurred to her. "But all's not lost on the radar screen! We'll keep on driving, driving, driving till his old rubber pecker gives up trying. Oh yes. Oh you thought, didn't you, that it would be like Miss America in a bathing suit in the snow. A mountain in the snow. But it's bloody. You are bloody. It comes out between the cracks. Slow like it's melting."

She leaned across the table then and FJ could smell her smoky coffee breath when she whispered, "Believe me. Just do believe me. You're still just a little girl at heart, but you should know enough to believe me. Our blood is melting all the snow."

And FJ didn't know what to say to that so she picked up her menu, then thought of something and said, "Say Janice, you know I left the house without a dime. I didn't know we were going out for breakfast."

"Going out for breakfast! Is that what we're doing?" Janice let out a whoop of laughter at the idea, and other people turned to stare. She reached in her bag and pulled out a man's wallet.

"Taken care of. On me, on the house, on your brother's goddamn blood-soaked house. It's all the same, money. Where it comes from. Order what you want." She shook a lit match at the menu. "Have an ice cream soda and a hamburger if you want! Out for breakfast!" She leaned back and dissolved in a fit of laughter.

FJ went ahead and ordered scrambled eggs, and she was a few bites into them when she again remembered her aunt's remark about the medication. She thought about saying something, just a casual question about whether Janice needed to take any of her pills or anything, but just then Janice's expression changed. The dim light of the diner seemed to be too much for her. She shielded her eyes with her hand and sank into the booth, and with a cigarette dangling from her lip she said in a whisper, "I guess you know he beats me up." And FJ stopped eating and put down her fork.

Back in the car, FJ felt afraid for the first time that morning. It wasn't Janice's driving; they were cruising through the little town at a nice safe speed, and Janice seemed calmer than she'd been in the diner. But still FJ had the feeling they were moving far too fast.

"If it's all right by you, kiddo, I believe I'll head back onto the highway. The American interstate system is a miracle, don't you think? All those miles and miles of road and it's up to you to keep it going. If you want to you can drive and drive forever. You never have to stop."

FJ cleared her throat and started to speak but stopped. Then she opened her mouth again and said, "Well what about going to the bathroom?"

"Well, yes, the bathroom, gas—but then it's all in your control. What I'm trying to say is, there is then no demonic red light or eighty-eight sided sign to flash in your face and terrorize you and say stop *now*, not when you want to or you need to, but *right now*."

"True, true," FJ nodded, very much wanting Janice not to get too excited.

"I don't know about you but there is something about an eighty-eight sided, fire-engine red stop sign that can almost make me weep. Because I'm just afraid of what might happen."

"If you stop, you mean?"

"Yes, if I stop. For too long." Janice grabbed FJ's hand then and held it. "There have been times, little one, when I have stopped my car at a red stop sign and just looked at it and thought to myself, well all right, I've stopped, and what now? I've just sat there at that stop sign feeling like I'll never move again, and in fact I may not even remember how to breathe once I let out the breath I'm holding onto right now, and . . . ." Her eyes glazed over as her voice trailed away; she seemed to forget what she was saying.

Then suddenly Janice turned back to the road ahead. "Put it this way, squirt." Her voice had more of its earlier edge, but she kept on holding FJ's hand. "It's important to keep moving. You've got to, if you want a chance at staying off their radar. Stay away from stop signs. They might look harmless but they're wolves in sheep's clothing. There for our safety my ass—they're traps."

And then there it was again, FJ's roommate's dried-out washcloth, dusty blue with frayed edges. FJ thought suddenly of Berenice and caught her breath. From the time they'd moved out of the house in town and Berenice had quit working for them, that year after the awful scene at the wedding and after her cousin John Henry died, the year FJ turned thirteen and left something behind, almost like an umbrella or a pair of gloves but harder to put a finger on than that, she'd hardly thought of Berenice and John Henry at all. She simply hadn't let herself think of them.

But during the first semester of her freshman year of college she cried herself to sleep at night with a queer sort of longing for both of them, for the housekeeper from her childhood and a snot-nosed little boy with bad eyesight. They were all she had in the world, her audience and her counselors for all those endless summers until she turned twelve, until the summer when she threw herself at Janice and Jarvis's feet after their wedding, begging them to take her with them, to take her anywhere—a scene so shameful to her that it seemed in the end there was nothing to do but turn thirteen and get on with things, to turn her back completely on the child she had been. On Berenice and John Henry. On all their talk and dreams. Even on her own name. She spent her high school years in hiding from the brazen, disgraced girl she'd been as Frankie, and then at seventeen enrolled, in a kind of sleepy fog, at the state university campus near her home.

Each morning that year, jerked back to the cold reality of her sterile freshman dorm room, she opened her eyes and stared straight ahead at that God-forsaken, dried-up washcloth. She had never seen her roommate actually carry the thing to the bathroom, though clearly it had been used at some point.

During the entire second semester she and her roommate might have spoken five sentences to each other. FJ finished the year with a C average and without ever calling Berenice, though she'd thought at times—often alone at breakfast in the early morning—of doing so. Now, at the beginning of August, it wasn't clear whether her father would be paying for her to return to college, and it also wasn't clear that FJ even wanted him to.

He beats her up, she thought then; she says he beats her up. And FJ wondered why it was that she believed this desperate, manic woman immediately, almost instinctively—that she didn't have the slightest doubt that this was true.

Cars were speeding by them. FJ looked at the speedometer and saw that Janice, who was lost in some thought or another, was going twenty miles an hour. She squeezed Janice's hand tighter and looked out her window at the patches of brown grass.

In her dreams of college she had walked from left to right on the movie screen of her mind, over lush green lawns and into ivy-covered buildings, to hear scintillating lectures about Michelangelo and Tennyson. But in fact the buildings were new and the desks were scratched with graffiti and she walked from right to left over hot concrete most of the time. In her classes she watched filmstrips and dozed. There was not a single college party—the boys all drunk and red-faced, the girls rolling their eyes and pretending to be stupid—that she'd enjoyed, and every time she went to the library she grew frightened for some reason, and she felt an overwhelming need to go to the bathroom.

Now she felt as unmoored and bewildered as she had ever been. For the time being though, sleeping late into the summer mornings and spending the afternoons on a chaise lounge in the back yard with a novel had been a way to forget about it all for a while. But now here was Janice, talking crazy and driving worse, bringing it all back with her eighty-eight-sided stop signs and her hacking smoker's cough and a husband, FJ's own brother, who beat her up. Yes, of course FJ knew what Janice was talking about. She'd been held up at one of those bright red road markers for the better part of a year.

Gradually she realized that Janice had begun to cry.

"What is it, Janice?" she asked her then. "Are you okay?" And she patted the hand that held her own.

But Janice yanked her hand free then and slapped the air where FJ's hand had been, "No, I'm not all right, I'm loose as a goose, I'm a firecracker ready to go off, a loose cannon aimed at the outer zones of the universe. If I can just get there, if I can just fly a little farther out, I'll be off their screens for good. You'll see, kiddo, I'll fly right off the map and then they'll never get me back."

"Who?" FJ asked, even though she knew Janice had to mean Jarvis. And for FJ there was her father, Aunt Pet. Everyone who seemed to like her best when she was quiet and out of the way. And hadn't she once talked about a similar feeling with Berenice and John Henry, seated around the kitchen table with the playing cards spread out in front of them? Everybody feels caught, she had said that day (and she winced, remembering Berenice's reply—"I'm caught worse than you is"). But to her it seemed more like everyone—and most of all she herself—was coming loose.

"All of them, the psychiatrists, your brother, my parents, the whole bloody shebang," Janice said as she grabbed her open handbag off the floor. For another cigarette FJ assumed, but instead she pulled out a bottle of pills.

"It's these, squirt. Watch out for these things." She shook the brown bottle, rattling it in FJ's face. "They'll pin you down with these." She threw the bottle in FJ's lap.

"It's this they're after," Janice went on, pointing at her right temple. "It's the top that's spinning up here, spinning so hot and fast they can't get a hold on it, but not because they aren't trying, oh no. I'm spinning right out of their grip but they're desperate to get to that hot spot at the middle. The tropical zone. The psycho-tropics."

Janice giggled then, pleased with her pun, and FJ laughed, too. "The psycho-tropics," FJ repeated. "That's clever." She put the bottle of pills in her shorts pocket and said, "I hate to tell you this, Janice, but I have to pee."

This was true, she did in fact have to pee, but besides that, FJ was getting very nervous. The more Janice talked about her spinning top of a mind the faster she drove. Yes, FJ did remember feeling loose, too, when she was a kid. But right now the fact remained that at the line about the psycho-tropics, FJ looked over to see the speedometer needle coursing well beyond the speed limit, to sixty, seventy, eighty, and beyond. And at that point she looked closely at Janice and admitted to herself that yes, in fact, she felt afraid of being as loose as that.

But by this time Janice was mumbling to herself—more about not stopping, about what might happen if she did—and it was clear she'd forgotten FJ was even in the car.

"Not this time!" she hissed as ashes from the cigarette at the corner of her mouth drifted onto her skin-tight T-shirt and the bare, downy skin of her arm.

"Not. This. Time." By now her voice was barely above a whisper, but she pounded the steering wheel furiously with each word.

And even though Janice had taken her foot off the accelerator now and the speedometer needle was on its way back down, FJ knew that all she could do was close her eyes and brace herself, grit her teeth and hope for the best, because like it or not, Janice was flying somewhere else right then and it didn't matter whose car it was or who was in it. So that when they rolled off the highway and finally smacked into a tree, the only thing that surprised FJ was the silence afterwards. In those silent seconds she had time somehow to think of Luxembourg, the time when Janice and Jarvis were going to be stationed in Luxembourg, and it was a pale, pale blue in her mind, cold blue like ice, and she had a picture of Janice in a blue dress and blue shoes, the palest baby blue—the same baby blue as FJ's brand new set of Samsonite luggage, packed and piled in the corner by the door the night before she left for college, and the same sad baby blue, she realized then, as her roommate's stiff, dry washcloth, hanging so forlornly on the back of their dorm room door. Still hanging there today for all she knew.

FJ heard a whimpering then and looked over to see Janice hunched over the steering wheel, her shoulders shaking, her long, thin arms covered with goose bumps. Sweaty wisps of hair curled over her ear and a faint blue vein showed through the soft skin at her temple. She looked, FJ thought, like a little girl.

"Janice?" FJ said.

Janice looked up at her and blinked. "He's gonna kill me now," she said. Her voice sounded small and hollow.

Later, when a policeman arrived, they sat on the slope above the road. Janice was still sniffling, and FJ stared at the crushed front end of her brother's Firebird and tried to see the blue she'd seen before, but couldn't. As the officer got out of his car and lumbered up the hillside she fingered the bottle of pills in her pocket.

He'd just opened his mouth to say something, probably to ask, "Y'all all right?" but before he could get a word in, FJ blurted out, "It's all my fault. My daddy won't let me get a driver's license so I begged her to let me drive my brother's car and now look at what I up and did." And she shook her head and rolled her eyes and tried to look remorseful, but because she knew she'd long since lost the skill of lying like an actor on the stage, she finished up by burying her head in her arms, which she'd wrapped around her sweating knees.

The policeman didn't say anything for a minute, and FJ could feel his and Janice's bewildered eyes staring at her, but she kept her head down and her eyes closed until the policeman finally cleared his throat and said to Janice, "Well, all right then, ma'am, do you reckon we can find the registration and insurance and put in a call about this?"

For just a second Janice sat there, and then she pulled herself up to her knees. FJ turned her head a tiny bit and watched through squinted eyes as the policeman helped her up. Then, before she walked over to the car with him, Janice reached down and put her long, thin arms around the tight little ball FJ had made herself into, and she kissed FJ on the top of her head.

"Lovely little Frankie," she breathed in FJ's ear. And right then FJ felt strong enough to hold the whole world in place with her very own arms.

When they'd walked away to the car FJ pulled her head up ever so slightly and reached back into her pocket for the bottle of pills. She pulled off the top and poured them out there on the hill, and seeing those bright green pills in the red Georgia clay made her think of Christmas, of a whole other season in a whole other place, cold air and the smell of pine and the heat of a thousand or so candles. Christmas in Luxembourg maybe, or anywhere at all. She could go anywhere at all, she thought.

She smoothed two handfuls of dirt over the little pile of pills and pulled herself up from the ground then, and she walked over to join Janice and the policeman beside the Firebird. Seeing Jarvis's new-to-him Firebird in such a state made her want to laugh. But remembering her role she held it in, and she worked to make her face look sorry.

Everglades City

INGE PUSHED HER ANGLED BANGS AWAY FROM HER EYES TO examine the sign more closely.

"Alligator handlers work for tips."

"*Was macht* 'tips'?" she asked her companion, Judith, at top volume, momentarily forgetting that they were watching a serious performance: in the fenced-in pit before them, a dark-skinned and dark-haired man in blue jeans and narrow-toed boots was gently patting a large female alligator's belly, making soft cooing noises like you would make to a baby.

Judith glared at her, visibly annoyed. She was much more sensitive to American customs and expectations than Inge was, and as a result, Inge—who tended to ask questions loudly, always at the wrong moment, and who struggled to retain the odd American English expressions that Judith seemed to grasp so readily—was constantly, repeatedly embarrassing her friend.

"*Trinkgeld*, Inge—like in the restaurant, what we put down for the server," Judith hissed at her. "Now be quiet and watch."

The dark man who was cooing to the alligator had noticed them by now, and Inge braced herself for yet another peevish American sigh and visibly annoyed American stare.

31

But instead the man smiled up at them. His strong teeth were brilliantly white, and they lit up his deeply tanned and dimpled face. Inge found herself smiling back and, she realized, probably blushing a little.

Uncertain about the American custom for tips for alligator handlers, she left a five-dollar bill in the small aluminum bucket below the sign perched on the fence surrounding the pit. Later, while they ate lunch with other German tourists at the hamburger stand across the highway from Captain Jack's Alligator Show and Boat Rides, the alligator handler, whose name was Mike, asked Inge and Judith if he could join them at their picnic table. When she realized that in his case Inge would definitely not need her help, Judith excused herself and said she would see Inge later in their room.

So this was how it all began—Inge's romance with Mike the Seminole alligator handler in Everglades City, Florida and, ultimately, her decision not to return to Cologne with her friend Judith, a hairdresser, at the end of their three-week Florida tour in the spring of 1993. Instead she stayed on in Everglades City with Mike, in his little frame house on Frangipani Street, walking three blocks in the morning to the little grocery store in search of something decent to cook for his supper that night, choosing not to think about the life she'd left behind in Germany.

"I hope you know what you're doing," Judith said—a characteristically patronizing parting shot—as she boarded the bus in the hotel parking lot on the day the tour moved on to Miami, leaving Inge behind.

Some nights Mike brought home a bag full of the local stone crabs and a little plastic jar of mustard sauce, and they would sit on the back steps of his house, cracking open their dinner with a wooden mallet, laughing as they fed each other juicy bits and licked the mustard from their fingers.

She hadn't guessed that fish and beer could taste like that—tangy and salty, like her own sweat—or that she would be able to give herself up so completely to the wet and languid heat of a Florida spring. Nights with Mike left her happily numb those first few weeks. Cold air from the tiny window air conditioner above his bed blew across their bare, sweating stomachs as he stroked her like the drowsing, mindless animal that she felt herself becoming.

She was happy then, and most of the time at first, but at the end of her second week with Mike, he came home with a red gash on the inside of his forearm from the mother alligator at Captain Jack's ("barely a scratch," he'd called it). Then early the next morning, walking along the edge of the Barron River, Inge came across a dead anhinga, its head curved almost modestly below an unnaturally bent wing. And gradually, a strange, unnamable feeling, a mix of restlessness and anxiety, began to seep through at the edges of her new hot, green world.

Often when Mike got paid they would go out for a special dinner at one of the two sit-down restaurants in town. "The nice places," Mike called them. One Friday night at The Rusty Anchor, the nicer of the two nice places, in Mike's opinion, Inge decided to try to speak to him about her fear.

"I want a knife," she said. "One like yours."

She sat across from him in one of The Rusty Anchor's big vinyl chairs on wheels, fighting the impulse to slide in and out from the table—something that, while relaxing and pleasurable for her, seemed to irritate Mike. Though she'd been in Florida for a month by this time, she still could not bring herself to eat the fried pieces of bread the local people called hush puppies. Maybe because they were named after a small dog. She rolled one back and forth across her plate absentmindedly, slowly saturating it with tartar sauce and lemon juice, while she tried to gauge Mike's reaction.

"What do you need a knife for, Inge? You're not training alligators." He drained the last sip of his Rolling Rock and started taking bites from her plate.

"No—not for the alligators, Mike. For the, how to say this, for the danger. For protection from the danger here. Like in the newspaper today."

In that morning's *Miami Herald* they had seen a grainy photograph of the murdered victim of a carjacking—a young German man of twenty, with blood pouring from the side of his face. They'd both stared at it at the breakfast table, sipping orange juice, as Mike prepared to go to work.

"That picture was taken a million miles from here, Inge. On the outskirts of Miami, remember? That's a whole different world from Everglades City."

In her mind Inge tried to imagine what Mike meant by "a million miles." From her map, she knew that Miami was approximately 100 kilometers away, and the conversion to miles was always difficult for her. On top of that she assumed, from his tone, that Mike was speaking figuratively, but this was often difficult for her to recognize, or understand.

It was hard to concentrate. Behind her she heard the waitress, Bev, a friend of Mike's, speaking to another table of German tourists.

"Virtually all pompano fish are caught in nets," Bev said, and the German tourists nodded hesitantly.

"What means 'virtually'?" Inge wanted to ask her. "You should not assume they will know what you mean."

"Listen, Inge," Mike was saying to her, taking her hand and pulling her eyes back to his. "You don't need a knife. You've got me—I'll protect you."

He stroked her hand and smiled his brilliant white smile at her, and Inge felt the same thing she'd felt that day at the burger stand with him, the feeling that made her decide, impulsively and recklessly, not to return to Germany with her friend.

She smiled at him then and lowered her eyes. "All right, Mr. Big Protector," she said, and they both laughed.

But in another corner of her mind, Inge was already planning ahead, thinking that she would have to handle this on her own, some other way. This was something she often did—thinking in separate boxes like this. It was, she knew, how she'd made the decision to stay in Everglades City in the first place.

It was Judith's idea to spend their spring vacation in Florida, and Inge had said "All right then, but not just the beach. I want to go to the swamplands; I want to see the alligators."

Judith had sighed resignedly, then agreed, knowing her friend well enough to decide not to argue. Inge was a kind and lovely person in many ways, Judith said to her that day, but also odd; her interests would have made sense in a man, but in a woman they were peculiar. She seemed to prefer feeling frightened to feeling pampered, and she made impulsive decisions. Like the silly one-sided haircut she'd insisted on before they left.

"I want to stand out," Inge had said in response, only a little hurt by her friend's bluntness. "I don't want to look like a typical German."

"For the alligators?" Judith asked as she snapped on the plastic cape and began, as she always did, as everyone always seemed to do, to give Inge what she wanted.

This despite the fact that, as Judith muttered under her breath while she clipped that day, Inge did not need a lopsided haircut to stand out. Tall and lean, Inge looked more Scandinavian, or maybe Icelandic, than German, with her white-blonde hair and narrow, cat-like green eyes. She dressed in black, even in the Florida heat, and favored short, tight skirts over her traveling companions' more practical cotton shorts. But she tended to wear them with baggy, faded T-shirts, a combination that created a jarring but clearly appealing effect, at least to men: an intriguing blend of sex and shyness.

She *was* odd, probably, Inge thought. At least compared to Judith, who was mostly patient with Inge's oddness, and also with her attractiveness to many men. There had been many occasions when Judith had risen from a table in a restaurant or bar, leaving Inge to her conversation with some man who'd decided to join them. She was used to making a graceful exit, as she'd done that day at the picnic table with Mike. The only thing that had given her pause that day, she told Inge angrily, turning on the bedside lamp in their room when Inge returned hours later, was Dirk—Inge's fiancé, back in Germany.

Judith had agreed to a week in the Everglades, since the trip was, after all to be a celebration of Inge's completion of her two-year apprenticeship in the insurance company—the company she was supposed to return to, for a full-time position, at the end of the spring vacation. But at the end of the week Judith boarded the bus for Miami Beach alone, and Inge put her career in the insurance company on hold, as Americans liked to say.

This Inge had learned from Mike. "What do they mean, your friends, when they say to me, 'What do you do'?" she asked him during the first week. "I want to say that I do many things, but I believe that they think there is something wrong with me because I live here with you but I do not have a job."

"Just say your career's on hold," Mike told her. "Just tell them you were in the insurance business in Germany, but that's on hold right now and you're deciding what to do next."

So this is what she said, in the weeks to come. She liked the expression "on hold," the way it seemed to say that if you wanted, you could simply make time stop for a while. Lots of people in Everglades City seemed to be doing that. Moving slowly, if at all. Working just enough to pay the rent and buy food and beer, surrendering wholeheartedly to the heat, the strangeness, the deep, musky smell of fish and salt and pungent blossoms—a smell that seemed to reach its peak each night near dawn. Inge had breathed the smell in deeply and then held her breath, joining Mike and his friends in an endless summer cycle of growing restless and frustrated, then drinking and fighting, then making up with a passion that left her panting and exhausted.

She'd joined them completely, or nearly so. They were all on hold, all waiting, though maybe, she thought, they'd forgotten what they were waiting for. How long can you put your life on hold? Inge wondered, and again the unnamable feeling came over her.

Since she was a child Inge had wondered why everyone around her seemed so fearful, so averse to taking risks, and since her teen years she'd been alarmed by the same growing tendency in herself. Green Party activists in their youth, her parents had settled into a safer, more comfortable life after her birth, as had most of their friends. And they now had serious, respectable business connections—hence Inge's position at the insurance company.

"It's something in the German psyche," a teacher of hers at *Realschule* had said once—driving Inge to rock and roll boyfriends, short black skirts, complex body piercings. "We follow blindly, we don't take chances." She'd never forgotten that, and she'd never stopped battling her own fears and hesitations. A job in the insurance industry was wrong in every way.

The day after her conversation with Mike in The Rusty Anchor, she'd changed her mind about the knife, deciding on a different plan. Every afternoon at three o'clock a young man Mike knew, named Woody, came to the basketball court in the park across the street from Mike's house with a six-pack of beer. Inge watched him as he drank one can of beer, then shot exactly five baskets from five different positions, then drank another can of beer, sweating and looking around him through his narrowed eyes and the strands of long hair he kept brushing away from them.

One day she asked if she could join him. She had been a successful center when she was at *Realschule*, and he seemed surprised by how good she was. It seemed silly to her to make small talk, so after they finished a ten-point game, which she let him win, she said, "In America it is very easy to buy guns I believe, yes?"

She had heard this, of course, before she came to the United States. Everyone in Europe knew about the easy availability of firearms in the U.S., and when she arrived in Florida and saw all the gun stores in shopping malls along all the nameless highways, she realized just how true this was. The giant store on the edge of Everglades City was called Big Al's Guns and Ammo; she'd stopped to look in the window one day on her way back from the Post Office.

Woody stared at her through his hair-draped eyes. "Easy enough if you're willing to pay." He bounced the basketball twice. "What're you looking to pack?"

What means "pack?" Inge wondered, but thought it better not to ask.

"I have money—I can pay what is needed," she said, and pointing to the lone remaining Budweiser in its plastic ring she added, "Also, I will buy more beer for you if you would like."

"Sounds good to me," Woody said, and he bounced the ball twice more and threw a jump shot that missed the basket completely.

"I'm thinking revolver," he said then, looking Inge up and down and nodding knowingly. "A nice, neat little revolver—it'll fit in the palm of your hand."

And Inge thought to herself how odd it was—though not particularly surprising to her at this point—to hear an American speaking about a gun with such obvious affection. With something approaching love.

Americans loved peculiar things. Cold beer drunk from cans. Food that was fried. Boats and big, rangy sport utility vehicles. Animals. Their love of animals might have been the most peculiar of all. Mike's neighbor, Mrs. Ames, fed her ancient tiger cat Lindy with a spoon every morning after Mr. Ames left for his boat. Another of Mike's friends, Larry, had a pet anaconda for which he received weekly shipments of live mice as food. Inge assumed this was because as an American, he objected to capturing and killing mice on his own, but Mike insisted that no, first of all they had to be alive, and second of all they weren't that easy to find in the waterlogged Everglades.

Instead there were alligators, thousands and thousands of alligators, and in truth, Inge was disappointed and confused by this animal. For while busloads of tourists waited in the blazing sun for entire mornings for sightings of alligators in the nearby parks and preserves, less than a mile away there would be a farm where other alligators were raised like cattle, and if those tourists wanted, they could order alligator to eat that night at dinner.

And then there were the trained ones. The big sleepy mothers and sprightly youngsters, alert to every move of their handler's shiny blade. Gentle, almost purring, surprisingly soft to the touch, only now and then baring their teeth, happy to be stroked and fed and lying in the sun. Much like the locals, Inge decide—calm and relaxed on the surface but with their weapons sharpened and ready, hidden just below the surface.

Though Mike remained consistently gentle, both with the alligators and with her, Inge had seen another side to certain of his friends and acquaintances in Everglades City. Fights broke out at the height of most parties, and in the dead of night a woman's voice might pierce the darkness, screaming and sobbing with rage. And once Inge saw one woman, a waitress at a bar at the edge of town that Mike had instructed her never to visit alone, pull a knife on another woman at the end of someone's fishing dock. Everyone else (except for Inge) kept on drinking and looked the other way, and eventually the two women embraced, collapsing in tears and falling into the river, still ignored by everyone on the bank.

"It's crocodiles that are dangerous," Mike assured her the first day she accompanied him to work at Captain Jack's. "People always get them mixed up." The Seminoles had a long tradition of playful wrestling with the alligators, he explained, and even though Mike was actually only one-quarter Native American, he preferred spending his days with alligators to spending them on a fishing boat, or worse, on one of the loud, motor-driven tourist pontoons that coursed up and down the river all day long.

The way he touched them reminded Inge of the way he touched her. It was both tender and menacing. Or perhaps the glinting knife blade she thought she saw, or felt, while he stroked her own belly or traced a patient, shivery circle around her nipple, was only the product of her overheated tourist's imagination. It was her choice to stay, to put her career "on hold." And—something she hadn't yet managed to mention to Mike—to fail to explain, to a waiting German fiancé in Cologne, her absence on the group's return flight to Frankfurt.

"I hope you call Dirk," Judith said that day from her perch on the bus's step. But so far Inge hadn't done so.

It was pleasant to forget, to float through the sultry Everglades City streets, soaking in her own glistening sweat, to watch delicate orchids and bougainvillea and poinciana blooming overnight—big drooping blossoms of red and orange that looked hot to the touch and spread a blanket of sweet smells over the whole town. To cook fresh fish on Mike's little charcoal grill, holding a cold, sweating bottle of beer to her forehead, and to fall, hot and flushed and always a little drunk, into his arms, his bed, undeniably aroused by the hidden blade. Wishing she had one of her own.

Instead she'd have to settle for a gun. The next day Woody brought her the revolver he had promised, a Smith and Wesson Ladysmith, and, just as he'd said, it fit neatly into her palm. It weighed only ten ounces—less than 300 grams, Inge calculated— and suddenly she wished there was someone German with whom she might share this astonishing piece of American data. Woody showed her how to load the bullets, but when the lesson was finished, she emptied the cylinder and returned them to their box.

"I really only want to have it to hold in my hand sometimes," she said.

"Gotcha," Woody said, and seemingly as an afterthought he added, "But you know for holding in your hand, there's nothing beats a 357 Magnum. I saw a beauty in Big Al's yesterday—marked down to $450."

He wiped the sweating strands of dirty blonde hair from his eyes, and Inge watched as they fell immediately back over his forehead.

"You should get a haircut," she said as she reached for the wallet in her knapsack, thinking that she could, perhaps, offer Woody some advice as well. He wasn't exactly bad-looking, though he could stand to play a more rigorous game of basketball from time to time: all those cans of beer were beginning to go to his belly, and he always looked like he needed a shower, which seemed unusual for an American. He'd been fired from his job as groundskeeper at Captain Jack's because, Mike said, of his inability to get to work by nine AM.

"A haircut, a shower, not getting drunk by five o'clock every day," Inge continued, pointing at the empty plastic rings that had held that day's six-pack. "Then you could maybe keep a job and keep yourself looking better."

For a moment Woody looked stunned, possibly hurt, and Inge realized, once again too late, that she had exceeded another American boundary that she didn't understand. But then Woody seemed to perk up, and pointing a finger at her, he said, "Listen, I'm not sure you're one to talk, little miss German girl," he said. "Who is it that's left a job back in Germany and is living off her American boyfriend here in the U.S., huh? What exactly are you doing to be such a big contributor to our fine American economy?"

She didn't know how to answer the question. She had a sense that Woody was right, that he was understanding her situation all too well, and for just a moment she wished Judith was with her to explain what she should do or say next. *What means "contributor"?* she thought but didn't say. Then she remembered Judith's advice as they boarded the bus in Tampa—when in doubt, just say you're sorry—and she opened her mouth to do just that, but before she could say anything Woody went on.

"Okay, maybe a haircut. Maybe I ought to clean up a little bit. I'll give you that. But if I do it'll be for my own reasons"— and he pointed an accusing finger at her again—"not because some smart-ass German tourist thinks I ought to get a job. Got that?"

"Smart-ass" wasn't a compliment, that much was clear, and Inge decided then that rather than apologize, perhaps she ought to change the subject. So she reached for her bag and pulled five one-hundred-dollar traveler's checks from her wallet. "Come with me to cash these," she said. "We can go to Big Al's, and then with what is left we can go for you to have the haircut."

She left him at the barber shop on the way from Big Al's that day, and instead of one more revolver, she returned to Mike's house with two new guns. Big Al himself (who winked aside the fact that Woody was obviously shopping for guns of behalf of a visiting tourist) made the offer, approaching them as they stood discussing a specially-marked Colt 45. He waited patiently as Woody explained the relative merits of automatic vs. semi-automatic pistols, and while he waited he twirled the cylinder of a shiny, used .357 magnum. When Woody finished, Big Al offered Inge both the Colt and the used magnum for a mere $600.

It was too good to pass up, Woody insisted. "That's damn near as good as two for the price of one," he said, and Inge shrugged, then nodded, pulling an additional traveler's check from her wallet.

The irony of what she was doing was not lost on her. It wasn't that she didn't have the money; she did—she'd been saving for this celebratory trip for quite some time. But these were dollars that were meant for Miami Beach, for Palm Springs, and for a three-day jaunt to Puerto Rico (Judith had mailed her a postcard from Old San Juan). Instead, Inge was using all her carefully saved money to buy guns, for reasons even she didn't understand.

But she didn't want to go to the beach. That much was clear. She liked it better here in Everglades City, in the remote and swampy Everglades. The beach made her think of Dirk, of his plans for their honeymoon. His plans, not hers—he wanted to go to the Bahamas. The beach was boring to her, she wanted to tell Dirk, just as she'd wanted to tell him so many things but couldn't. And they even spoke the same language.

Inge and Woody had spent so much time in the store that day that she had to race to get home in time to stash her new purchases in her duffle bag, stuffed to the rear of Mike's closet, before he got back. The next morning, after he left for work, she brought the bag out and sat on the edge of the bed in her nightgown, gently handling each of the guns one by one, rolling the smooth bullets in her palm, squeezing the trigger and emitting the sound of a small explosion from between her puckered lips. It was all very soothing, she decided, and before long she was thinking about the rows of shining shotguns on the rear wall at Big Al's. They gleamed like the flanks of horses, she thought, so shiny and new and American. Her duffle bag was just long enough, she decided, to hold one.

The haircut may have been a mistake, Inge thought that day at the basketball court, though she chose not to say anything about it. With short hair Woody looked even more overweight.

"I have been thinking about the bigger gun that we saw at Big Al's yesterday," she said as she dribbled. "What was the name of it?"

She passed the ball to Woody, who shot and, of course, missed. "You mean that pump gun? They called it something like 'The Persuader,' I think. Yeah, that was it—The Persuader." He dribbled a fast circle around Inge and went in for a lay-up that, surprisingly, landed in the basket.

Inge winced then, remembering the rack of guns she had seen next to the sinister black Persuader. "Youth Rifles," the sign had said. Guns for children. She stopped dribbling and held the ball.

"It is so, how to say this—so *irrational*, this American habit of guns!" she said, surprised by the outrage in her voice. "First they make guns so easy to buy—for anyone, anywhere at all. And then they make special guns for children!" She stared at Woody, as if demanding an explanation.

He held out his hands and waited for her to pass the ball before he answered. "So who said Americans were rational?" he asked, then threw in his second basket—the first jump shot Inge had seen him make.

"You're the rational ones, you Germans," he continued. "And look where that got you. Ready to take over the whole globe and kill half the people in it in the process."

This Inge understood. She was prepared for it, for references to the war. It will happen in America, friends and family had warned her. He is trying to change the subject, she told herself, to avoid my question about children and guns. "This does not answer what I asked you," she said. "Why are there 'youth rifles'? What possible reason could there be for Americans to sell guns for children?"

Woody shrugged. "Kids like to hunt," he said, and he passed the ball to her. "So what? So Americans aren't rational. But at least we're free." On that note he tried another jump shot that went familiarly wide of the mark.

"Anyway, if you want a shotgun, I've got a better idea." He went on talking, granting her, as usual, the last shot of the day. And the next day Inge found herself driving with Woody to a vast armory building in a small town forty miles away. It was her first, and last, gun show, and she came home that day with an AK-47. No questions were asked of her, and the man who sold it to her accepted her traveler's checks without even asking to see her ID.

Yes, it was irrational; she was infuriated by all of this—and yet the guns she purchased were a strange and undeniable solace. She might, in fact, have begun to feel quite calm and accepting of her on-hold life as she approached the end of her second month in Everglades City, except for one new problem: Mike.

As time passed they seemed to find each other less interesting. More and more often he called to say he was going out for drinks with his friends after work, and more and more often Inge felt that she didn't really mind when he did. He was thinking of buying into a business with his brother—an alligator farm. He thought it was time he settled down, bought some property, a bigger boat. She was beginning to think that she had this effect on men: they became suddenly more responsible, got haircuts, got serious jobs. And Mike was even putting on weight from all her good cooking.

The same thing had happened to Dirk. A musician in a rock band when she met him, he had since discovered that his true talent lay in the selling of musical instruments and equipment. As a result, he'd recently grown far more acceptable, as a partner, to Inge's parents, and far less interesting to her. Judith always took Dirk's side, seeing her chronic restlessness, Inge knew, as hopelessly spoiled and immature. Which, she knew, she probably was.

Because now here she was again. With a man who wanted to settle down, with whom sex had become lifeless and routine. Maybe it had something to do with how safe his work with the alligators was, really—as he kept insisting every time she tried to speak of the danger. The only time he got hurt, he said, was when he was being careless. Really, he said, they weren't much more than farm animals. Cows with big teeth. Which was why the real money lay in raising them, not training them to entertain the tourists.

The first day at Captain Jack's she'd been transported back to her childhood, to the circus, to lion tamers, acrobats, swallowers of fire. And for her first few weeks in Everglades City, Mike, with his taut body and perfect white teeth, his deftly handled silver knife blade, had seemed to embody all that was wild and daring and colorful and so, so different from her safe and tidy German life. But now, suddenly, he always seemed to smell of cigarettes and stale beer, arriving home sleepy and indifferent. Suddenly he seemed as well-fed and domesticated as anything else raised for public consumption—perfectly suited for handling a fat mother alligator that only opened her satisfied mouth to yawn.

And while she continued to find Woody, who remained in chronic need of a shower, rather repellent physically, it was undeniably true that, despite difficulties with language, her conversations with him were far more interesting than they ever were with Mike. But there she was, still living with Mike, trying to remember what it was that had made him so compelling.

And then there was also Bev, who'd entered the picture in a complicated new way that, Inge thought, seemed too elusively American for her to understand. Had she and Mike always flirted so obviously at the restaurant, at bars, at parties? Or was this something new?

"What is your relationship with this woman Bev?" Inge asked Mike one night, arriving home from a party where he'd had considerably more to drink than she had.

He finished yanking off a boot and fell back against the row of pillows on the bed before looking up at her where she stood by the closet door.

"What do you mean, our relationship?" he slurred, staring at her through watery eyes. "We don't have a relationship. She's just Bev; I've known her since we were kids." And before Inge could try to word her question more precisely, he had closed his eyes and begun to snore, one booted foot hanging off the side of the bed. Even drunk and asleep he was fastidious about protecting the bedspread. His neatness was one of the things Inge had admired about Mike, but now she found it mildly irritating.

She pulled off the remaining boot and threw it deliberately onto the pillow beside his head before pulling her duffle bag off the closet floor. Outside, sitting on a lawn chair beside the back stoop, she watched the light from the bulb beside the back door gleam off the revolver's handle, resting there in her hand like a kitten. She could almost hear it purr.

When she felt herself staring to doze, she carefully returned each gun to the duffle bag, quietly pushing it to the back of the closet floor again. That night she slept on the sofa in the living room, and when Mike rose early and crouched beside her to ask what was wrong, she only shrugged and smiled at him sadly.

"It's the language difference, I think," she said. "I think we are having trouble talking to each other now, and maybe it is because I don't know how to tell you things I need to say."

He stroked her hair and kissed her lightly on the forehead

before heading into the kitchen to fix his breakfast. And for just a moment Inge remembered that what had made her stay here, in this house in Everglades City, wasn't only Mike's muscles and teeth and shiny silver blade. It was his gentleness too, the sweetness that made him so calm and affectionate with the baby alligators, clucking at them like a mother hen.

But despite all that sweetness and all that strength, there was, Inge knew, something between them now. There was no getting around it. She felt bored. Once again, her life seemed safe and parched, lacking any interest, any risk.

When she heard him finish his breakfast and take his plate and cup to the sink, Inge closed her eyes and pretended to sleep, but in fact she was thinking about what she might do. All day long it rained, and she walked to the grocery store during a humid lull in the late afternoon. As she stood at the pay phone outside the store's front door, a swarm of tiny gnats descended on her bare, sweating shoulders and neck. She held the receiver in the crook of her neck, dialing with one hand and batting uselessly at the sticky cloud of bugs with the other.

Much to her surprise Dirk had acquired an answering machine. The sound of his voice—cheerful, confident, full of authority—made her heart sink, At the sound of the tone, she hung up.

That night, two more German tourists were shot, this time at a twenty-four hour gas station outside Orlando. It rained every day for a week, and the bugs settled in to stay. Suddenly Everglades City seemed empty and hauntingly quiet. In the grocery store she heard someone say, "Well, I guess all the Germans will just stay home now. Pity. My husband just got work repairing boats at Captain Jack's."

Everyone grumbled and groused about the rain, the insects, the lack of tourist money. Everyone but Mike. Every day he left for Captain Jack's promptly at eight o'clock. There were three new alligators just in for him to work with.

"They'll be back," he said, with complete assurance and serenity, about the tourists. It was the first sunny day after a full week of rain. "You oughta see these beauties, Inge—why don't you come to work with me?"

He looked a little worried when he asked her that. It was true she hadn't left the sofa very often that week, and most nights he'd had to eat pizza or go out for dinner with his friends. But going to work with him turned out to be a big mistake.

Watching him stroke and mew at the baby alligators that morning, Inge felt something inside her snap. Kind of like a door slamming closed—but also like a frayed piece of rope that gives in to too much weight and pressure. Still she hadn't spoken to Dirk, who now had an answering machine and, presumably, a new life. Two days before she'd received a frantic letter from her mother, demanding to know a return date, reminding Inge of the very real possibility that she could be forfeiting her chance at a good job with the insurance company—not an easy thing to come by in Germany these days, she hoped she didn't need to remind her daughter.

But worst of all, it had been days, no weeks actually. Actually weeks since Mike had touched her that way. The way he was touching the baby alligators with his silky left hand, while his right hand held the shiny blade next to their closed mouths and open eyes. When she couldn't bear to watch it any longer, she turned around and walked to his house. Not aimlessly this time, though. Perhaps for the first time since she had arrived in the United States, maybe for the first time in her adult life, she was walking with a purpose, with a plan. It had to do with her duffle bag but not with a tiny revolver she could hide in the palm of her hand. No, for this she needed the weight and strength of that horse of a rifle Woody had helped her pick out. Walking home, she tried to remember the steps for loading, cocking, and firing the thing.

Early in her stay she had found them. A mother and two babies, hiding among the mangrove roots in a small inlet, well off the tourist path at one end of the Big Cypress National Preserve. Earlier, when she was happier, she would bring a water bottle and her camera and walk to this quiet spot in the morning after Mike left for Captain Jack's. She would sit silently for an hour or so, until eventually they emerged from the murky edges to sun themselves on an exposed log. Sometimes they were joined by a giant turtle which, when the mother got too close, would pull its head and arms tightly into its shell, making Inge laugh silently to herself, envious of that ability.

She had shot five rolls of film at this spot. But that day, after watching Mike with the baby alligators, it wasn't her camera that she carried in the heavy duffle bag she threw over her shoulder.

How could she make sense of a place like the Florida Everglades? Dark, ancient, rich with smells and dampness and every conceivable size and shape of living thing. A place where anyone at all could buy a rifle meant for war, where guns were sold especially for children, where there was one set of laws protecting one set of animals, and another set of laws protecting the citizens' rights to kill a different set of animals in whatever way they chose.

Every time she walked deep into the grounds of the preserve, these questions nagged at her. At the same time, she noticed a subtle change in her own breathing, in the way her own body smelled to her. Deep, certain calm laced with a touch of panic. The way all the tensely sleeping animals must have felt. It was, she knew, the strange, unnamable thing that had kept her in Everglades City all this time. That restless anxiety. Now, not even Mike could soothe her. Something had to give.

Of course she had no intention of shooting the mother. On the other hand, she still wasn't sure what she was doing there, shaking uncontrollably with her rifle loaded, cocked, and aimed, when suddenly she heard a noise to her left, jumped in fear, and shot the waiting bullet into the silent mangrove trees.

The only sounds, then, were the echoing explosion and the splash of alligators diving off the log, as she turned to her left to see sunlight glinting off of metal. But this time it wasn't a knife blade, or a gun. It was the badge of the national park officer at the gate, the one who came by from time to time to watch the alligators with her. This time, though, he arrested the pretty blonde tourist from Germany with the funny haircut, and when he asked her what she thought she was doing, she said, "Perhaps it is that I do not have the language. But I do not really know."

Benedicta

ARTIST'S STATEMENT

The painter Van Lloyd, discouraged about the prospect of revolution, has decided on his final subject. We are entering the final round of realism. This is his last chance to get it right. Revolution now has a new, distinctly female form.

NAME (in bold or larger font)

Choose a professional spelling of your name and stick with it. If you have the exact same name as an artist who's already garnering attention, consider a variation. This might be frustrating, but it also might lessen confusion.

Richard Riesman (1978-1986)
Richard Van Lloyd Riesman (1986-1989)
Richard Van Lloyd (1989-1997)
Dick Van Lloyd (1997-2000)
DVL (2000-2001)
Van Lloyd (2001-2009)
The Painter Van Lloyd (2009-20?)
Benedicta (20?-)

CONTACT INFORMATION
Preferred mailing address, phone number(s) (work/studio/home), fax, e-mail address, website. If a gallery gives you a show or chooses to represent you they will probably eliminate your address, phone numbers, etc. This is because they want potential buyers to contact them directly regarding any interest in your work.

Good! Fine! The Painter Van Lloyd has never owned his own place! He has mainly lived and worked in borrowed garages and cheap rented rooms! This was, for a time, connected with his fame!

Now he sleeps and works, Monday through Friday, in his first wife's ex-husband's weekend house. On the weekends he trolls the streets of San Francisco, looking for models. Young women today don't look like they did thirty years ago, which is a problem. Nor do they smell like the girls of his past; these young women trail behind them the scents of their shampoos and creams, their various elixirs. Save for the sleek long hair on their scalps they are hairless as newborn mice. They drink bottled water. Their edges are smoothed and leveled by pharmaceuticals so they can finally stop washing their hands.

But honestly, though he has been accused on several occasions of never having advanced beyond the age of twenty himself, his interest in these girls is purely professional. He says this and means it, no winking. He is looking for someone even remotely close—in her physical honesty, in her high seriousness, in her lack of self-consciousness—to his girlfriend Benedicta. Who has told him that after the birth of her child, after a year or so—now stretched to two years—of devoted care to this new being, "we will see."

EDUCATION

M.F.A.	1989	Painting	Yale
B.F.A.	1986	Studio Art	UC Irvine
B.A.	1984	Philosophy	UC San Diego

SHORT BIOGRAPHY

Born: year and city/state or city/country
Work/Live: city/state or city/country
Note: The absence of such information suggests that an artist might be hiding something.

Born: 1961, San Diego, CA
Work/Live: Stinson Beach and San Francisco/California/U.S.A.
But before this there was

San Diego/California/U.S.A., where The Painter Van Lloyd surfed and painted and read Freud, Nietzsche, quantum physics. Paintings here were mainly of friends, fellow surfers and students, and were distinguished primarily by some skill with line and human form, plus an attitude of alienation and contempt conveyed on faces that were always cut off by the boundaries of the canvas. None of these paintings was sold, and none survives.

Yale/New Haven/Connecticut/U.S.A. Graduate school. When his interest in realism (unnamed and unexamined as it might have been) quickly became, in the eyes of others and then his own, a sign of a quaint, West coast-ish ingenuousness. Immaturity, provinciality. He would come home from the "pit crits" at Yale to lonely, bleary-eyed Linda and screaming, four-month-old Peter, hunkered down in their freezing basement apartment, with nothing left for either of them. What in God's name were they doing there? Who did he think he was kidding?

An MFA from Yale? Right. He belonged on a beach, with a surfboard.

It was Linda—jealous already, though at this point her jealousy was groundless—who said to him, "Well for God's sake why don't you just use that surfer boy persona here? They might not like your work but it's clear they all think you're gorgeous, some kind of Greek god Beach Boy. I've seen them at the bar. They *all* want you, the women *and* the men." She lifted her shirt and attached her screaming son's mouth to an angry red nipple. For a fleeting moment The Painter Van Lloyd longed to draw her and his son, but he suppressed the desire to capture this sad and lovely tableau in front of him. Mother and son. He closed his eyes and shook his head. Too romantic, too much realism, they would laugh at him, who was he trying to be, Norman Rockwell?

And so he assumed a de Kooning-esque persona—the raving California Dutchman, blond and tan and shirtless—and began to paint cartoonish breasts on slabs of concrete, the left breast always labeled *perfervid*, the right *sacerdotal*; he had discovered that the emeritus professor who taught his first art history course at Irvine used one or both of these words in every article he published. And then he moved to. . .

New York/New York/U.S.A. . . . . and began working with women's underwear and shards of glass. Work which was deemed somehow Parisian, though he hardly knew Paris, having spent only two nights there, in the summer of 1984, until he ran out of money and got back on a train with his Eurail Pass and backpack, and headed to his younger sister's student apartment in Amsterdam. Where he spent his days sketching in *Vondelpark*, until he had completely exhausted the sympathy and additional funds of his sister and her punk-inspired friends.

And thus returned to California and went to art school, married his first wife Linda and fathered their son Peter, dragged Linda and newborn Peter to New Haven, then installed them in a gritty Long Island City apartment in Queens, shared a studio with some other Yale MFAs in Williamsburg, and made disturbing, supposedly Parisian things out of cheap white underwear that he bought in packages of a dozen in Chinatown.

In New York in 1990, to have chosen torn white lace underwear, to have used the cotton crotches as canvases for the tiniest landscapes, done all in reds, was to be perceived as a reader of Foucault, a *Discipline and Punish*-style liberator, a mod deconstructor. By the time, years later, when—as Dick Van Lloyd—he displayed a tire sculpture resembling a labia and titled it "Many Who Claimed to Have Read Foucault Were Lying," the critical perception had shifted. And he had become known not as a liberator, but as a hater, of women.

The artist might be hiding something. Well, yes. If the critical perception of his work was going to be less about the work than about his life (the divorce from Linda, the dalliances with European models), then perhaps it was time he hid. In Europe, behind some aviator sunglasses, in some borrowed leather. If it's all artifice, then it's all artifice after all. The sculptor Dick Van Lloyd, heir to the conceptual artist Richard Van Lloyd, born of the never fully committed abstract expressionist Richard Van Lloyd Riesman. In Europe, as Dick Van Lloyd, he created rubber tire remnant constructions: the aesthetic of the American highway, with undertones of NASCAR.

But now: now what would he possibly have to hide? Two ex-wives and, at present, a girlfriend in Brussels. His son Peter now in London, where he makes a comfortable living representing the tire remnant sculptures and sees his father, begrudgingly, twice a year. (It is Peter who has suggested that he put together this artist's resume.) Yes, in the past he did carry on a ten-year flirtation with conceptual art that wasn't, in truth, very conceptual. Blunter than that, in truth. After the red landscapes came his signature white underwear with lace, this time dirty and bloodied at the crotch, glued, along with pieces of broken beer bottles, to slabs of cement. These sold, but he was too engaged in a protracted series of battles with Linda—who had taken Peter back to California with her; who found him lacking as both a husband and a father; who would have liked for him to come home once in a while, for God's sake—at this point to have seen any of that money. When they divorced, she moved to San Francisco, and he went to Prague.

In Prague he reveled in his status as an "outsider artist," which required that he hide his training, along with his ex-wife and son. Relics of another life. He dressed like a biker, torn denim and distressed leather, reeked, always, of cigarettes, claimed not to have finished high school in the U.S., and happily leered at women. Retrieving vestiges of torn rubber from Czech highways—dodging all those wheezing Skodas, like so many tiny, lunging beetles—proved difficult, which further enhanced his image. Dick Van Lloyd, the madman American. Brando of the roadway and the gallery, happily inhaling all those deadly fumes as he glue-gunned rubber to rubber.

He quickly put together work for a group show, called "Palimpsest: Beneath the Surface," held in a cavernous underground space below a seventeenth-century monastery. He enjoyed this very Czech-sounding title ("Beneath the surface lies . . . nothing!" Raucous laughter and the clink of shot glasses). For this, besides the signature tire fragment sculptures, he brought in more underwear, glass, and cement. At the opening, he met Gizella, who was Slovakian, and who had him hold her glass of pilsner while she deftly removed her thong and handed it to him, "for using maybe in your next great work." He kept it in his pocket for quite some time instead. They married, and he returned with her to New York in November of the year 2000. At which point America had begun to grow stranger than anyone thought possible.

He was now affixing hunks of hair from roadkill to tire fragments to canvases, signed only DVL. Gizella—long-legged, pouting, spooky Gizella—quickly acquired some of his old New York habits (an interest in the company of someone, anyone, other than her mate, a failure to come home very often) along with some of her own (a fondness for heroin). And while many chose to marry in the wake of the Sept. 11 attacks, he and Gizella chose to divorce. Gizella left for Prague on the first flight she could get out of New York; he watched the crumbling, smoking debris from the rooftop of a friend's building abutting the Brooklyn Bridge. And left soon after for Amsterdam.

With his notebook of sketches from the summer of 1984. In which was one of a dark-haired girl, a gypsy girl of his imagination, rendered there in her lacy camisole, long arms open and extended, dancing. Arabic? Romany maybe? Long hair loose and eyes closed, intent with concentration. Surely, for this was Vondelpark, stoned. While someone, probably her boyfriend, in torn jeans and flannel shirt though it was hot, played a guitar, badly.

He decided, on his return to Amsterdam in 2006, that he wished to paint one last series of paintings: portraits of this gypsy girl, this anti-Joni Mitchell. And then one day, on the Rembrandtplein, he happened upon Benedicta, soon to be his Belgian girlfriend. She could have been the girl in Vondelpark, except that, as she pointed out to him when he pulled out his notebook to show her, she was not yet born that summer he drew his gypsy girl, his belle *Hollandaise*. Benedicta painted as well—large, dark canvasses. Unutterably bad, as she knew. She invited him to move in with her, and she allowed him to photograph her, right up to the moment of her baby's birth in the spring of 2007, there on the pile of cushions in the middle of her nearly empty Amsterdam flat, midwives at hand on either side, while her bourgeois parents, who seemed rather bored, drank tea in the next room, awaiting their opportunity to pack their daughter's remaining things and then whisk her and their new grandchild to the inn they ran outside Brugge.

The look on Benedicta's face, there in the quiet moments between the seismic contractions of her body, was the look of the dancer in *Vondelpark* years before: so avid in its focus, eyes so still yet so alert. Her body was fuller, lusher than he could have imagined, a fruit ripened beyond recognition, a flood bursting a levee. Her long brown hair, that waterfall of reckless curls, was wet and streaming.

But the photographs have failed to capture all of this, and so he must rely, also, on his memory. Every brush stroke here is crucial.

And because this type of information seems valuable for some reason, and because he would not wish to be accused of hiding anything, The Painter Van Lloyd would like to note that the child emerging from Benedicta's transformed body at that moment was not his. He had met Benedicta only four months before. "When it is ready, this masterpiece you are imagining, you will sign it with my name," she told him early in her labor, between contractions. "And then you will be taken seriously at last."

GRANTS AND AWARDS

His records here are sketchy. There were a few New York Council for the Arts Fellowships in the early and mid-nineties, an NEA grant in 1992, a one-time grant named for Vaclav Havel and handed to him, in the form of a check that appeared to be signed by Frank Zappa, in a smoke-filled bar sometime near the end of the previous millennium.

SOLO EXHIBITIONS AND GROUP SHOWS, COMMISSIONS, COLLECTIONS

Records here are similarly deficient. Following the Yale Thesis Show in 1989, there were several shows at the Great Jones Gallery in Soho, a group show at the Brooklyn Museum in 1994, the "Beneath the Surface" group show in Prague in 1999, another group show with a less interesting name that he's forgotten at the Lazarus Gallery in London in 2000. Records of his work as Dick Van Lloyd and DVL, including information on collections holding these works, are available from the Painter Van Lloyd's son, Peter Reisman, c/o Bremmer Gallery and Design, Inc., London.

ARTIST'S STATEMENT, CONT'D.

Here some history of the nude in more recent Western art may be in order. First, the Painter Van Lloyd's choice of title, "La Hollandaise," is a play on Walter Sickert's nude of the same name—named for a character, the prostitute known as "la belle Hollandaise," in a Balzac novel. When he was young and sketching in Vondelpark, when he was Richard Reisman, the Painter Van Lloyd discovered Sickert and the Camden Town painters, and he fell in with their dark visions of the lower classes. Their realism. Who, at 22, let loose in a hashish-rich park in northern Europe, would not be drawn to a painter some writers would later claim, in complete seriousness, was Jack the Ripper? It was Benedicta who reminded him of this, saying, "And so I am your *belle Hollandaise*?" But he told her no, this is something else entirely.

Sickert, who admitted he was repulsed by most traditional compositions of nudes, finding them like a "dish of macaroni, something wriggling and distasteful" hid his prostitute's face in a swirl of hostile brush strokes. This was akin, Van Lloyd thought—after he was DVL but before he became the Painter Van Lloyd—to his own smeared underwear and cement constructions. His younger man's assumptions about Linda, whose pregnancy he'd largely ignored, about Gizella, about others. It isn't true that he'd hated them. What is true is that he had, for some reason, simply failed to *see*.

But what does his life story have to do with any of this, really? And why would his life story lead to charges of misogyny? He does not hate women. As a younger man, he may have appreciated too many, too much. But now he is simply, like so many artists, plagued by his inability to capture them in his work. Their clothes, flesh, fluids, focus. That tiniest passage for the largest of voyages. Van Lloyd was his mother's last name; yes, it's true. He has chosen it for most of his career, over that of his father, whose career was as a Naval officer. A cold, distant man whose violent center would occasionally boil over, brushing up against the edges of his skin and then receding; he would turn red-faced and tight-lipped, raise his hand, then leave the room. In fact the Painter Van Lloyd, little Richie Riesman, would have preferred to have been slapped.

He has never slapped his own son, who was raised by Linda and her second husband Anthony, an English designer and

gallery owner. As it turns out Anthony is gay, but never mind—
and yes, you're right: why must he persist in being snide about
his ex-wife's subsequent loves? What right does he have?

His son is also gay. And a very fine manager of his father's
work, though most of his money comes from other artists
who are represented by his stepfather—owner of the house in
Stinson Beach. Linda's second divorce was amicable, and now,
remarkably, they're all good friends. Now, when the Painter Van
Lloyd occasionally travels east for the holidays, he joins Peter,
Linda, and her third husband Frank for very civilized dinners,
which he honestly enjoys; Linda and Peter are excellent cooks.
What he thinks, now, when he is with them—and this is true,
not hiding anything—is this: what a wonder, that these kind and
cultured people remain connected with him. That one even, in
fact, shares a portion of his own genetic material.

He has never hated Linda, even at their worst. His own
mother, Patsy, was a sweet woman, pretty and shy. And yes,
of course, when she was younger Linda reminded him of her.
Patsy had dreamed of being a singer. Music, however, jangled
his father's nerves. The Painter Van Lloyd was eighteen when
Patsy died of ovarian cancer.

But speaking of women and the history of portraiture, let's
consider Thomas Eakins. Now there was a portraitist. Happy
to get naked himself, if that would help his model feel more at
ease. Poor fellow; where, in nineteenth-century Philadelphia,
were the beautiful, upper-class women who would take off all
their clothes? Now, of course, that's not the problem; it's the
alarming robot-like quality, the brutal sameness of those lean,
sculpted bodies that could drive an artist mad.

Ben Shahn said that Eakins loved "the incidental beauty of
things, but even more the actual way of things." The Painter Van

Lloyd has only recently discovered Ben Shahn's *The Content of the Form*. His reading now is as random and undisciplined as it was when he was twenty. As are his teachers and his influences. For instance, no one should be guided in life by a trembling, alcoholic proprietor of a store specializing in crystals in a beach town north of San Francisco; the Painter Van Lloyd knows this. And yet he can't help himself: he listens to Fred, the crystal store guy, as they drink coffee at the diner on the beach every morning, and he somehow believes what Fred has to say. The revolution will come. It has its roots in ancient legends. This wisdom has preceded us by millennia. We will be nothing but spectators.

Except he doesn't wish to be a spectator. And he now believes the revolution will come when we understand, at last, this one pure instance of beauty: a woman's legs parted, her cervix widened beyond recognition, for the passage of a human head. The moment, and the site of a woman's body, that we have all learned, instead, to fear and yes, even loathe.

We are in dire need of revolution. The birth of Benedicta's child has taught him this. But he can't simply wait for it to come, doesn't trust that what Fred is seeing, there in the bottom of his drained coffee mug, is what he, the Painter Van Lloyd, wishes to see.

Which would involve, perhaps, his mother singing. Linda swimming at Mission Beach when they were teenagers. Benedicta crowning. Which would have more in common, maybe, with Van Eyck. Giovanni Arnolfini's wife, Eve in the Ghent Altarpiece. Or Van der Leyden's St. Mary Magdalen. Better yet: in Van Eyck's miniature illumination for the Turin Book of Hours: The Birth of St. John the Baptist. Women, pets, all those domestic details. A clean bed. Everybody ready and waiting, and not a man in sight.

Because if, in fact, he hates anyone, most honest appraisers of his work and his life would have to agree that it's men.

Or better perhaps: the painter—also early Dutch—known only as the Master of the Female Half-Lengths, who painted at least twenty Madonnas, all ending at the knees or above. The Painter Van Lloyd might be, then, the Master of the Female Full Frontal.

In the Painter Van Lloyd's final, largest canvas, Benedicta will be crowning. Such a perfect term for this view of the baby's head there between her legs. In studies he is working on now, using the photographs from that May morning in Amsterdam, he has her reclining on a pile of Marimekko print-covered cushions, in an otherwise empty Amsterdam apartment. There is an element of Fauvism in this one stroke of bold color. Also a nod to Vuillard and his mother's dressmaker's shop in the attention the Painter Van Lloyd has paid to the pattern of the print.

But the only influence that interests the Painter Van Lloyd now, in a garage on a cliff above the Pacific in Stinson Beach—nearly three years into what will be, he is convinced, his final project—is that of the early Dutch painters. His heroes, Van Eyck and Van der Leyden. Whose life stories are unknown. Who of necessity have hidden everything. Whose biographies make no difference. Who painted with the accuracy he aspires to and will pursue until his death.

What he envisions is an altarpiece, for a twenty-first century church of the body. A series of smaller panels, then—images of Benedicta walking, Benedicta dancing, Benedicta sleeping. It's for these images that he needs models, though he never finds any. He's really just passing the time on those weekend walks through San Francisco, after he's walked Anthony's terriers and watered his plants. Passing the time until he can return to Anthony's weekend house, to the garage where he paints. Walking the streets and reliving the day he met Benedicta in Amsterdam, tottering in her silly heels and short skirt, staring into windows, eating a sandwich and not at all interested in him. She was tall and so aloof, and she smiled at him and rolled her eyes when he asked if he was correct in assuming she was pregnant, and also perhaps an artist? Neither perfervid nor sacerdotal, she reminded him of something about his younger self. His much younger self. Pre-Yale. If there are young women like her on the streets of San Francisco, he cannot see them.

Realism, in a ridiculous age, is revolutionary. A mother giving birth. A woman of indeterminate race. In need of no one. Benedicta, la belle hollandaise. Call it a mother obsession, call it regret. But understand that he intends for this work to be as free of his own psychology as it can possibly be. Form equaling content, his own St. Benedicta, her body and her child. The actual way of things. Signed by her.

Each weekday morning, after toast and coffee with Fred and a walk on the gray, rock-strewn beach, the Painter Van Lloyd uses Anthony's computer to send one e-mail message, to Benedicta in Brugge. In this message he reports on the progress he has made in his work, then asks if he might one day join her and her child, a daughter, bringing along his canvas for her appraisal and, perhaps, her signature.

And each night, before he goes to sleep, he finds the same reply from Benedicta: *Keep painting*, she writes. Then: *And we will see.*

The Beauty of Their Youth

AT WHAT POINT DID MUSEUM PLATES START TO SAY THINGS LIKE this:

During a challenging period the Athenians used these constructions to laud their own superiority and to publicise their divine ancestors and the beauty of their youth in an effort to justify and vindicate their overt imperialism in the Aegean.

Fran could have done without the "overt imperialism" part. Because of course it was this plate—not the perfect statue of Herakles, glowing in the room's filtered sunlight—that her daughter Miranda had chosen to photograph. When exactly had it started, this habit of her daughter's of aiming arrows directly at the heart of all of Fran's passions, her own youthful joys? It feels like Miranda's been doing this practically from the time she was born. Not a difficult child, and also not a difficult adolescent or young adult—Miranda was just a smart, observant, and relentlessly critical one.

"Like her mother really," Fran's husband Jeff would say. Has said.

She and Miranda were on the Greek island of Delos, in the Archeological Museum, where photography was permitted. Like everyone else, Fran and Miranda had their phones out, snapping away. So far Miranda, who'd turned nineteen that summer, had spent much of her time staring at the row of stone lions. Fran was working hard not to follow her daughter around and gauge her reaction to every object, and also to tamp her own enthusiasm and all the things she wanted to say.

These lions are remarkable, aren't they? Particularly the way the light from those high windows hits them here. I think you see them better here than outside, though of course walking through those rows and rows of reproductions outside gives you more of a sense of what it must have been like, just the sheer vastness of it all, the brazenness, the display of art, and beauty—art and beauty and power. Imagine them being linked like that, imagine art mattering that much!

It came so naturally to Fran, to talk that way. To talk too much. She taught English at a private high school, and these were the kinds of things she said to her students during the unit on the roots of western literature. Her students seemed to find her enthusiasm sort of cute, a little wacky, the way you might feel about those kinds of enthusiasms in your mom. Or, well, in someone else's mom.

Miranda had just finished her freshman year at Barnard. This trip was a birthday gift for both of them, mother and daughter, from Jeff. Secretly, Fran was hoping to convince Miranda that there could be some value in studying abroad somewhere in Europe—in Rome, say, as she herself had done thirty years before.

But Miranda was noncommittal. "Maybe . . . ," she'd say, then trail off. Or, "I don't know, I don't think it would be like it was for you, Mom. I'd probably be in a dorm full of American students, taking classes and visiting the sites like any other tourist." If she studied abroad at all, Miranda has told her parents, she might consider a rain forest ecology program in Mexico that she's read about. Though even that felt kind of invasive, like plopping her big, American-hiking-boot-shod foot down in the middle of a fragile eco-system. "Global travel is just another form of imperialism," she'd said, quoting her first-year seminar teaching assistant, a brilliant young man she'd adored.

Later, in the museum cafe, they ate ice cream and shared a lemon Fanta. Fran thought Miranda's nose looked a little pink, maybe peeling a bit; she'd inherited her mother's fair skin, and Fran had foisted heavy-duty sunscreens on her from the day she was born. Now Fran instinctively handed her a tube, pointing to her own nose, and for once Miranda dabbed some on without an argument. Outside the cafe, Miranda stopped to pet a little swarm of stray cats, then paused to take a photo of a rusted old pay phone, clearly not used for years, the numbers of its key pad faded by sun and wind.

"Layers of empire, all turning to dust," she typed on her phone, then posted this caption online, along with an artful little montage of photos—some statues, the museum plate about the imperialist Athenians, the ancient pay phone. She showed the screen to Fran, who looked and laughed, though in fact the whole thing made her a little sad.

She'd been enchanted by Delos when she first visited the museum and the parched, sun-baked grounds, packed with more glorious antiquities than one could possibly absorb in a single afternoon. But that had been more than thirty years ago, in a different century, when she was a wide-eyed twenty-year-old. She'd stayed on for the summer after her semester in Rome, to work at a low-end resort on the island of Naxos. She'd gone to Delos with her Greek boyfriend Giorgos on one of her few days off, taking photos the way one did back then—choosing carefully, considering the bulk of the rolls of film, the cost of eventually developing the prints. She still had the photos from that long-ago summer somewhere, probably buried in a box in the attic.

Now she glanced toward the port to see their ferry approaching. Disappointed, she took her daughter's arm and pointed to the boat. She didn't want their time on Delos—which Miranda seemed to enjoy more than Fran had expected, even if it was for ironic, twenty-first century reasons—to end.

The resort on Naxos where Fran had worked back in the summer of 1983 no longer existed. But the place where she and Miranda were staying felt similar in certain ways. It must have been built around that time; everything had the look of the 1970s or 80s. Their room had a small kitchen and a separate sleeping loft on a second floor; everything was dark wood and scuffed marble. There were two swimming pools, both clean if rather worn around the edges; the beach, with its small, deep cove for swimming, was a short walk away, past a fenced plot where noisy goats were always eating something, though it was hard to imagine what on that dry, dusty plot. The farmhouse, like so many structures on the island, was unfinished.

The Greek economy had never been exactly booming, of course, at least not in Fran's lifetime. But they'd planned their trip at a particularly low point for Greek citizens, the summer of 2012, well into a season of out-of-control debt, a plummeting euro, austerity measures, raucous protests, and a bit before the first big wave of refugee boats.

"Interesting time to add Greece," was all Jeff had said, giving her a meaningful look across the breakfast table as she opened a map of the Greek islands.

The original plan had been Italy only, and mainly Rome, where they would visit Valeria and Carlotta, the daughters of the family with whom Fran had stayed all those years ago during her term abroad. Their father managed a hotel—the Hotel Cinecittá—that was originally owned by a wealthy and mysterious Dutchman who loved Italian cinema. Fran had recently reconnected online with Valeria, the younger of the two daughters, who'd been her good friend when they were both twenty. Before that there'd been years of silence. Not angry or disappointed silence, simply the drift of years, and distance, and difference that used to happen to everyone back in the days before social media.

From Valeria's Facebook page Fran learned that Valeria and Carlotta's father, Signore Moretti, had died, and their mother was now an invalid; it seemed that neither sister had married. But the hotel remained much the same, as did the small birreria, the Ristorante Utrecht, where Valeria and Carlotta still served breakfast in the mornings and drinks in the evenings. As they'd done since they were teenagers.

Except for that one summer, the summer after Fran's semester of art history and ancient civilizations classes in Rome, when she and Valeria met two Greek brothers, Giorgos and Kostas, and ran away with them to the island of Naxos. Or so the story went when Fran returned for her senior year of college, recounting her adventures to her friends.

Actually, Giorgos drove a truck and knew the owner of a hotel in Plaka, the hippie beach town, who needed summer help. Kostas worked for the small ferry company that shuttled tourists back and forth from Naxos to Delos to Mykonos, serving ice cream and snacks on a small, wood-paneled boat whose sound system played an endless loop of Burt Bacharach songs.

They'd met the brothers one night in the birreria. He enjoyed both the Netherlands—where he often made deliveries—and Italian cinema, Giorgos said, and so he and his brother had noticed the sign as they walked back from the Trevi Fountain to the Barberini metro stop. They'd lingered well past closing time, talking with Fran and Valeria. Carlotta had rolled her eyes and turned away and gone upstairs to bed. She'd been stern and disapproving since she was a child, Valeria said.

Fran had also reconnected with Giorgos online. Everyone, it seemed, was doing this. Even Carlotta had a Facebook page, though Fran had found no sign of Kostas.

While Valeria and Carlotta had only a few photos on their pages, mostly of guests at the hotel, Giorgos's page was filled with images of his family—the grown daughter from an earlier relationship, the teenage sons from his first marriage, the new wife and young children from his second.

From Delos she and Miranda took the ferry to Mykonos, now all high-end stores and restaurants designed for tourists, all white houses and blue trim and red bougainvillea, a movie set version of Greece. As they ambled back to the boat for the return trip to Naxos, a young man whizzed by them on an ancient bicycle: the snack bar tender, with a fresh bucket of ice. Fran smiled at the sight of him, remembering Kostas. The next day they would return to Athens for one more night, and then they would fly to Rome, where they would stay at the Hotel Cinecittá and see Valeria. How would she tell her about what had happened to Kostas?

He'd been the quiet, mysterious brother. Of course Valeria had fallen for him. Valeria, the reader of Henry Miller and Gabriel Garcia Marquez, the only member of the Moretti family who did, in fact, enjoy early Italian cinema. She was quiet and pretty, with long hair that she braided and big, dark eyes that always seemed to be searching for something. It was clear, as soon as Giorgos and Kostas struck up a conversation with the girls that night in the birreria, how things would go. Giorgos, the smooth talker with far better English, would go for Fran, the chatty American blonde; Kostas and Valeria would linger a bit behind them in the shadows, talking just a little, smiling shyly. Fran had been powerfully attracted to Giorgos, who was lively and handsome and charming. Yet throughout that summer of cleaning bathrooms and scrubbing poolsides during the day, then drinking Fix beer and dancing to Michael Jackson and U2 songs by the beachside bar until the middle of the night, she'd harbored a secret crush on Kostas, the dark brother, the brooding one, the watcher.

He was the first boy—man really—she'd kissed, Valeria told her. And Fran hardly knew what to do with her friend's innocence. When they announced their plans to spend the summer working in a hotel on the island of Naxos, in Greece, Valeria's mother had wept loudly, pleading with her daughter not to go; her father had closed himself into his office behind the hotel desk.

Back in the States, Fran's parents might have reacted in similar ways, had she not written a breezy postcard to them, explaining that she'd lined up good summer work in Greece, arranged through the study-abroad program. Lying through her teeth. She made up for her lies by deciding she would look after Valeria. Before they left Rome, she bought a box of condoms, sharing half with her.

She looked directly, and earnestly, into her friend's sad, dark eyes and said, "Make sure he uses these. Insist on it, okay?"

When Valeria nodded—so serious, so trusting—Fran had felt impossibly mature and ridiculously proud. Still, through all of that, she could see Valeria's fear.

"But you shouldn't do it at all if you don't want to, Valeria. You know that, right?"

Valeria had smiled at her then, a glorious, glowing smile. "I want to," she said, then nodded and said it again. "Yes, yes. I want to." And they both laughed, giddy with all that lay ahead of them.

For Fran, the adventure of that summer hadn't really been about sex; she'd already had sex, the fumbling, teenage kind, with a high school boyfriend who'd gone to the same college as she had. They'd broken up after their first year there, and no one had particularly interested her since. Not until Giorgos, the handsome young man who'd driven all over Europe, the clever joker, the one who took care of everyone and everything, who always had money, who smoked cigarettes like a French film star.

"He's still pretty hot," was Miranda's response when she saw his picture online, leaning over Fran's shoulder to get a look at her computer screen. And then, when she saw the picture of his young wife, she'd said "Whoa. She's even hotter."

She'd patted Fran on the back before she walked away, already bored by all the photos. "Don't worry, Mom. You and Dad look fine for your ages," she said, and Fran wondered what had brought that on. *Had* she been looking for reassurance somehow, in showing her daughter photos of the people she would meet in Athens in advance?

That was where they'd gone first. Giorgos, who now drove a cab, met their flight. He hugged Fran tightly, then kissed Miranda on both cheeks and held both her shoulders, gazing at her fondly.

"She is like you were!" he said, finally looking back to Fran. She only smiled and nodded, not bothering to argue. She knew her daughter was prettier than she'd ever been—a good three inches taller, with a more toned body (she'd danced since she was a child) and the sleek, long hair she and all her friends cultivated as if they were tending a garden.

Giorgos had aged well, like a well-kept European actor; he looked a bit like Marcello Mastroianni. He wore khaki shorts, a Hawaiian shirt, and sunglasses, and he drove them to his house, in the hills outside Athens, in just the way Fran remembered him driving thirty years before—fast, confidently, as if everyone else should simply wait for him or get out of his way. As somehow they always did.

His wife Eleni was beautiful and young, closer in age to Miranda than to Fran. She'd laid out a delicious lunch—thick yogurt in terra cotta bowls, the kind of sweet red tomatoes Fran had only ever tasted in Greece, grilled fish, pungent olives.

In the end Fran felt reassured by it all. Absurdly young second wife or not, Giorgos had become every bit as settled and bourgeois as she had, maybe more so. He and Eleni were even sort of religious apparently; at one point his friend the priest stopped by, joining them for a glass of retsina. And before they left that evening, Eleni had pulled Miranda aside to give her a tiny plastic baggie with a piece of cotton dipped in some sort of sacred oil, from the Monastery of St. Luke—to "bless her travels," she said. To Fran it looked like a little packet of ear wax.

When it was her turn to account for the last thirty years that night at Giorgos and Eleni's, Fran ran quickly through the story—returning to her last year at the University of Michigan, working for several years in Chicago, meeting Jeff in graduate school, moving with him and their infant son to New Jersey when Jeff took a job in New York, eventually settling into a tastefully restored Victorian in a sleepy college town in eastern Pennsylvania. Now that son, Ben, had just graduated from college and started his own job in New York, and their baby, Miranda, had finished a year of college.

"It seems like only yesterday that I was her age, getting ready to fly to Rome for my big adventure abroad," Fran said. Because that was what you were supposed to say.

In fact, it didn't seem like it was only yesterday. It seemed like the thirty years it had actually been. She was twenty pounds heavier. Her hair was only blonde because her hairdresser made it so. She and Jeff had settled into something resembling scenes in those prescription drug ads on network television at night, two good buddies at home in their empty nest, eating air-popped popcorn and watching TV. Her daughter humored her but had her own vision for her life, one that was very different from the path she, Fran, had taken. And of course that was the way it should be, but still Fran wished they could share more, wished for the kind of closeness she'd always imagined having with her grown daughter.

Somehow she'd never pictured herself as a version of her own mother, or her mother as Fran had seen her when she was young. Hopelessly old. Hopelessly out of touch. A random thought danced lightly across Fran's mind as she chattered mindlessly on—about the cost of the dumpy Brooklyn apartment Ben shared with his girlfriend, the trip to Ireland she and Jeff had taken the summer before—which was this: Did Facebook somehow make you think you would never be truly *old*?

Jet lag was seizing her, a sodden weight settling onto her, starting at her shoulders and the back of her head. Suddenly she wasn't sure whether she'd thought, or actually said, that last bit about Facebook.

"And what about Kostas?" she blurted then, shaking her head to try to clear the fog.

Giorgos and Eleni exchanged a look. "Oh, Kostas," he said. "We'll talk about him another time maybe. You look tired. Let me take you and Miranda to the hotel."

For the next few days they were tourists, climbing to the Parthenon, visiting the Acropolis Museum, strolling through the Agora. On the night before they were to leave for Naxos, they met Giorgos and Eleni and the two youngest children for dinner at a cafe near Syntagma Square.

Though she saw him first, approaching their table on the outdoor plaza with a motorcycle helmet in his hands, Fran didn't recognize Kostas at first. He was thin and gaunt, unshaven and disheveled, and as he walked intently toward them, she braced herself, assuming he was a beggar who was going to ask for money. Throughout the evening she'd watched the affable maitre d' gently steering various sellers of roses and plastic toys away from his restaurant's tables.

Why, she wondered, was he allowing this man free passage toward their table? But then Giorgos looked up to see him. He rose abruptly from the table and pulled the man aside, exchanging words with him that Fran couldn't quite hear. Eleni, she noticed, took the moment to distract her children with french fries from her plate, muttering something under her breath.

The man walked up to their table then, with Giorgos close behind, and he stopped next to her and held out his hand.

"Hello Fran," he said, and when she heard his voice and saw his eyes, still dark and mysterious, still somehow enticing, she knew it was him.

"Kostas," she said, standing to embrace him. He let her wrap her arms around him but only stiffened in response, barely touching her. He was nothing but skin and bones.

"My English . . . ," he said, then shrugged and grinned, revealing his ruined teeth.

Fran laughed nervously. "It's okay!" she said, and she pulled him over to meet Miranda.

"This is my daughter," she said, and Miranda rose to shake his hand—gracious, unflappable, betraying no discomfort, despite his dirty, acrid-smelling t-shirt, his unwashed hair, still dark and curly but now streaked with gray.

"He can't stay," Giorgos said from behind Kostas's back. "Somewhere he has to be." And with that Kostas gave Fran and Miranda a little salute and a sheepish grin and turned to go. Giorgos walked with him to the entrance to the group of outdoor tables, where the hawk-eyed maitre d' watched as Giorgos handed his brother money and patted him on the back, sending him on his way. Back at the table, he clearly didn't want to talk further about it. And no one asked.

Later, back in their hotel room, Miranda told Fran what she'd heard Eleni mutter under her breath. "She called him a junkie," she said. "It sounded funny with a Greek accent. But I'm sure that's what she said."

That, Fran thought, might explain why Kostas wasn't on Facebook.

One day during their time on Naxos, Fran and Miranda rented a car to drive into the mountainous interior of the island. Their first stop was the Church of Panagia Drosiani, an ancient Orthodox church where a service was in progress. Somehow, Miranda had known to wear a long cotton skirt, and she'd brought along a bandanna to tie over her head.

"But you'll have to stay out here, Mom," she said, pointing at Fran's bare legs in her shorts.

From her seat on a low stone wall—twenty yards or so down a path away from the church, where her bare legs and head could be safely hidden—Fran could hear the strange but beautiful singing from inside the church, a kind of echoing drone that might have come from a cantor, or a muezzin. Not what she associated with the music of the church. She watched the random assortment of people arriving for the service, climbing the steep path from a village below—old men and women, dressed entirely in black, young women with babies, men who snuffed out their cigarettes and crossed themselves as they entered the church.

Fran had tried, but failed, to understand the allure of religious practices and iconography. In all her years of travel, churches and cathedrals had always left her cold. Synagogues too for that matter. Another way in which she and her daughter were different; visiting this church had been Miranda's idea.

When Miranda approached her on the path thirty minutes later, she was glowing, her forehead smudged with something powdery. The priest had blessed her, she said. When she asked Fran to take her picture in front of the gate, the church's bell tower and cross looming behind her, Fran said, "Please don't post this. You don't want your grandmothers to see it." She closed her eyes and shook her head, imagining trying to explain the giant Byzantine cross behind her bandana-wrapped granddaughter's head to Jeff's mother.

Miranda laughed, grabbing her phone to look at the shot. "I have places to put it where the bubbies never go," she said.

Then "They're after you for some reason," Fran said, reaching over to brush the powder—was it incense?—from her daughter's forehead. "First the oil from the monastery, and now this." She laughed a tight little laugh. "You aren't thinking of converting, are you?"

They were walking along the steep path to the road, where they'd parked the rental car. When Miranda didn't answer immediately, Fran stopped walking and turned to her. "*Are* you?"

"*Jesus*, mom," Miranda said, rolling her eyes. "Are you serious?"

But of course she wasn't serious. Was she? Fran turned back to the path, muttering some sort of apology. *Of course, so sorry, don't know why I said that*, and so on.

Did other parents do this, she wondered, allowing Miranda to move ahead of her on the narrowing path, this rehearsing of the list of awful possibilities? All the things that might befall their children. It was something Fran had done since both of her kids were young. Obsessively at times, almost ritualistically, like some magical way of warding off any of those possibilities.

Lots of things were higher on that list than religious conversion, of course—though that was on the list for Fran, whose parents had bred in her a secular Jewish identity that was almost a kind of religion in itself. Kidnapping was higher, as was being seized by a crazed pedophile. Once Ben and Miranda were driving, the inevitable list of possible car accidents. Drugs (and here Ben had given them some cause for worry for a while there, a few years ago). Cancer, or another fatal disease. A psychotic break one day, of the kind that had befallen one of Ben's friends during his first year of college, a sweet-faced boy from the soccer team who'd shot himself at the age of twenty.

It was superstitious and silly, and Fran knew it, and that was why she'd never told anyone about her habit of running through the possibilities from time to time, maybe once a month or so. More frequently before big events: sleepaway camp, the first time they drove on their own, college, an entire semester, or even a year, spent studying abroad. Hopefully someplace relatively safe. Ben had opted for a semester in Turkey, and Fran had drunk too much wine and gained ten pounds during the four months he was there.

What a fool she was, she thought now, walking on an ancient stone path down a Greek mountainside. To think she could control any of it.

And how glib, guileless, insufferably naive and self-involved she'd been thirty years before, deciding it was fine to lie to her parents about her summer plans, and also fine to bring along the innocent Valeria, her *truly* guileless friend. At the end of that summer Fran and Giorgos had promised to write, and to find a way to visit, each of them knowing that both were unlikely; it had been a simple, carefree romance for both of them. But Kostas had broken Valeria's heart, meeting someone else on Plaka Beach midway through the summer, a large-breasted girl from California, and riding off on his motorcycle with her.

So he still rode a motorcycle. You're so lucky that didn't last, she would tell Valeria when she saw her, in just a couple days. You can be thankful to that bitch from California (how Fran had despised that girl, about whom she'd known absolutely nothing). He's a ruined man.

For the next two nights, their last ones on Naxos, Fran had nightmares in which she lost her daughter. In one, Miranda was five, the age she'd been when they *had* in fact lost her, briefly. It was during a family vacation, at a resort with a massive, and crowded, playground for the kids. They were there with Jeff's big extended family, a situation that always made Fran tense. And that year, there was more: Jeff had, she knew, slept with someone several months before, while she and the kids were in Chicago visiting her parents.

A mistake, a misstep—he'd been beyond remorseful at their sessions with a marriage counselor, pleading with her to forgive him. She'd think it was all okay, she had managed to forgive him, it was all over at last, and then something would happen, and she'd snap. On this particular occasion, it was the walk along the beach to the big playground, where she could see his two sisters, already there, heads bent together, talking, gossiping—about her, Fran assumed, and the other in-laws. They only trusted their four blood siblings, it seemed to Fran, and they made it clear that everyone else would always be an outsider.

Their kids were older, running wild and free, and Fran and Jeff had let Ben run on to join his cousins. But Miranda was still with her parents when the fight began. Probably Fran said something about the sisters—"Oh God, I can't face them yet, Jeff, not this early in the morning." And he'd probably said something innocuous, like "Come on, Fran, they're not that bad."

That would have been enough, in those days, when she thought she was over it but she clearly wasn't. She wouldn't even know what hit her, and then she'd be crying, raging, screaming at him. At some point, in the middle of it all that morning on their way to the playground, they realized Miranda was gone.

That was when everything turned—that endless, horrifying hour when they couldn't find her. Her brother hadn't seen her, nor had any of her cousins. The playground area was huge, maybe an acre or more of molded plastic swings and slides designed to look like animals, all of them crawling with children, all become nightmare creatures suddenly. They found a security guard, and suddenly two more appeared, all asking about what Miranda looked like, what she was wearing; in her terror, Fran recalled—still ashamed at the memory—she couldn't remember. And another shameful memory: In the midst of it all, she was sure she saw Jeff's sisters—also searching madly, also baffled and afraid—pausing to give her smug, judgmental looks. And she'd felt a wave of pure, nauseating hatred for them.

Jeff stayed calm and focused. He ran back to their room, searching everywhere. He sent Ben and the cousins to search the bathrooms, the snack bar. Fran, meanwhile, kept wandering aimlessly, eventually crying, then sobbing. She was on the brink of full-blown hysteria when she knelt down to look inside a slide that was painted to look like a caterpillar and caught a glimpse of Miranda's sneaker.

She'd climbed up to the darkest part of the slide, tucking herself against the edge so kids could get around her. She'd been sitting there the whole time, crying.

"Stop fighting like that," she said when Fran climbed up to her, clasping her little legs and laying her own head on her daughter's tiny lap, crying with her.

And they did stop fighting. After that, Fran had put it behind her. She'd forced herself to let it go, for her daughter's sake.

Fran and Miranda spent one more night in Athens before their flight to Rome, but they didn't see Giorgos and Eleni that night. They'd been relieved, they admitted to each other, when Giorgos told them that he and his family were leaving that day, to drive to the country to visit Eleni's father.

Now there was only this one other visit to get through, Fran thought on the ride from the airport to the Hotel Cinecittá in Rome. Though she'd looked forward to seeing Giorgos and Kostas and the Moretti sisters, all of them suddenly real to her again thanks to the internet, she now felt a quiet dread. Seeing Kostas like that, seeing what he'd become, had unnerved her.

And the truth was, though the Moretti family had been good to her in countless ways, they'd also been rather reserved, even secretive. They were unfailingly gracious to the guests at their small hotel. But they preferred to keep their own lives—which were lived on the hotel's top floor sitting room and bedrooms, in Signore Moretti's office behind the hotel desk, and in the tiny Ristorante Utrecht kitchen—private. Fran knew next to nothing about them really, she realized, and she wasn't sure she had the energy to run through the last thirty years all over again.

When they arrived the hotel seemed not to have changed at all. The same dusty, blood-red curtains in the rooms. The roof garden that looked out over terra cotta rooftops, with a glimpse of the Trinità dei Monti church, at the top of the Spanish Steps, visible to the west. Valeria and Carlotta were busy with breakfast in the mornings, but some nights they sat with Fran and Miranda in the empty bar, which was closed during the summer months, or in the office, chatting idly, yawning from their long, hard days. Fran felt distinctly uncomfortable with the whole arrangement; why hadn't she realized how odd it would seem, to be served breakfast by her old friend?

And why *was* that old friend still serving breakfast to tourists, still assisting her sister and tending to her mother, basically the same things she'd been doing as a girl thirty years before? Valeria hadn't posted much, but from the few photos and brief remarks in Italian Fran had seen online, it appeared that, beyond her mother's illness and her father's death, very little in Valeria's life had changed.

Her hair was short now, and almost completely gray. Carlotta's hair was jet black, presumably dyed, and styled, Fran thought, like a grandmother's. They would only have to work this hard for a few more weeks, they assured her, bustling behind the birriera counter at the espresso machine and gathering used plates and cups from emptied tables. Then, in August, they would close the hotel for a month and, like all sensible Romans, leave the city. Before his death their father had bought a small property, a tiny house and enough land for a vegetable garden, in Liguria. He'd hoped to spend his retirement there, tending his garden, caring for his ailing wife. But he'd died of a heart attack in the first year he'd owned it. So now the daughters drove their mother there when they could, rolling her into and out of a van in her wheelchair.

"*Buonasera*, Signora Moretti," Fran had said the night she and Miranda arrived, when Valeria wheeled her mother into the restaurant. Probably the old woman didn't recognize or remember her, Fran knew. But she wouldn't have blamed her for pretending she didn't, even if she did. Fran was, after all, the wild American girl who'd taken her daughter away that long-ago summer, dragging her to a wanton summer and the loss of her virginity and the breaking of her heart by a brooding Greek boy. Who was now a junkie.

Fran wondered about it all, alone in the birreria with Miranda after breakfast on their first day in Rome. Granted, she knew next to nothing about the European economy and the two sisters' prospects for retirement, and granted they *did* have an ailing mother to care for. But when they arrived Carlotta had told Fran that she and Valeria owned the hotel now; Max Klein, their father's Dutch friend since the time of the war, had left it to them in his will. So why were they still working behind the desk and in the breakfast room?

"I guess that's one thing you can say for the tourist economy," she said to Miranda. "It's given Valeria and Carlotta work, and a steady income." How many times on this trip, she was starting to wonder, was she going to say things she didn't really mean? She was already losing track.

Miranda barely nodded, glued to her phone as she rose from the table.

"Though it seems like they could surely sell the thing, or something. And not have to work so hard. I wonder why they haven't just decided to do that."

"Maybe they *like* working here, Mom" Miranda said, picking up her tray and pushing in her chair. Fran had assumed she wasn't listening. "You could just ask them, you know, if you really want to know," she added on her way out the door.

Fran said nothing. Because maybe they did like it there. It was possible to like, or at least accept, all kinds of things. Who knew that better than she did?

That evening, fresh from a nap and a shower, Fran walked downstairs to find Carlotta and Valeria showing Miranda photos on a dusty old computer in the office behind the front desk. They'd begun scanning some older ones, Valeria said, but it was a slow process and often, by the evenings, they were simply too tired.

Now Carlotta scrolled slowly through images of her parents in their younger days, both dressed in smart, 1950s-style suits and hats, and of Valeria and herself, wearing ruffled rompers and playing on a beach. And then suddenly there was one of Valeria and Fran, age twenty, hugging each other and smiling at the camera, standing by the Trevi Fountain. Fran remembered the day Carlotta took that photo, the morning after she and Valeria returned from Greece; Carlotta hadn't been able to hide her happiness at her sister's return—or maybe, Fran thought, at the fact that she, Fran, would be flying back to the States later that day.

Miranda gave a little cry. "You were both so young! And so pretty!"

It was true. Their faces were clear and open, their skin radiant from their summer on a Greek island. Valeria had taken her long hair out of its braid, and it tumbled round her shoulders in beautiful waves. That was the way she'd worn it every night during their time on Naxos. Fran remembered the stab of envy she'd felt one night, watching Kostas's fingers slide through those dark waves, pulling Valeria closer as they danced.

"Kostas loved your hair down like that," she said without thinking. And at that Carlotta yawned and said goodnight, heaving herself out of the office chair.

"*Buonanotte*, Carlotta," Fran and Miranda said simultaneously, dutifully. But Valeria ignored her sister, taking her place in the chair and continuing to scroll through the photos on the screen. She paused, momentarily, at one of a beautiful, dark-eyed baby, a girl with a white bow in her dark hair.

The child of some cousin or other, Fran assumed. Though through all the time she lived with Morettis, she never heard or saw anything of an extended family, which had struck her as odd; it seemed to her that all Italian families were big, sprawling, loud.

"Who is that?" she asked.

"It's my daughter," Valeria said without missing a beat. "Greta. She lived only fourteen months." Her voice, usually quiet but lilting, even musical, was strangely flat.

Fran had been leaning over Valeria's shoulder, peering at the screen, and now she instinctively stepped back. Her mouth was open, but her mind seemed to have gone blank. She could think of nothing to say. There'd been nothing about this daughter online; she was certain of that.

Miranda, who'd pulled a chair up next to Valeria's, looked at her now. "What happened?" she asked gently, while Fran stood behind them, struggling to find her voice.

The baby had been born with infantile Tay-Sachs disease, Valeria told them. *In-fan-tee-lay*. The Italian pronunciation made it sound like something lovely and innocent at first, to Fran's confused ear.

"You know about it? It is common in Jews, and I have the gene. Of course we did not know of this then. Now there are tests."

Valeria shrugged, then clicked to another photo of the baby, a bit older now, but terribly small. "Even so, what would I have done if they had told me this?" She shrugged again. "Nothing different."

Her voice caught then, and it seemed, for a moment, that she might cry. But when Miranda reached over to hug her she held still for only a moment, then pushed her away gently, turning back to the computer screen and clicking the mouse.

The next photos were of the little house in Liguria—a series depicting its renovation—and Valeria sighed as she scrolled through them listlessly. "That is all of Greta," she said.

Fran found her way to a stool in the corner of the room. She cleared her throat and braced herself to ask the question that, for her at least, was hanging there in the room, unsaid. *Who was that baby's father?* The pictures of Greta were clearly old. And they'd come right after the one of Valeria and Fran on the day after their return from Greece.

"Valeria," she said, surprised by the loudness of her voice in the small, cluttered room, "when was Greta born?"

Valeria swiveled toward Fran, and when she saw her face she shook her head and gave a short, sharp laugh. "Oh Fran," she said, "not when you are thinking." She closed her eyes and shook her head again. "I remember, you were afraid."

The relief Fran felt was silly, she knew. As if an unplanned pregnancy that long-ago summer would have somehow been her fault, or her responsibility.

Now Valeria turned back to the computer and reached to turn it off. "Kostas was her father, but it was some years after we were in Greece together." She turned to face Fran again, and rose from the chair. "We were married years ago. Did Giorgos not tell you?"

Fran stared at Valeria, speechless again. She shook her head.

"We didn't really talk about the past," she said as Valeria squeezed by her, pulling the key to the office door out of her pocket. When she told Giorgos they planned to stay with Valeria in Rome, he'd barely nodded, then changed the subject. Still the same Giorgos, Fran had thought at the time—only able to see, or care about, what was right in front of him at the moment.

Kind of like her maybe, Fran thought as she stepped into the tiny elevator, squeezing in between her friend and her daughter.

Or at least like her younger self. Had she even known the Morettis were Jewish?

But of course she had; that had been the thing that reassured her mother when Fran announced her plan to study abroad in the land of the Vatican. She'd known the Morettis were Jewish, but she'd had no particular interest in that fact, other than the bargaining power it gave her. When they lit the Shabbat candles behind closed doors on Friday evenings—force of habit, Valeria had told her, since her parents' early years in Rome, after the war— Fran had seized the opportunity to go out drinking with friends.

And actually it might be open to question, how much she'd actually changed in the intervening years. Hadn't she spent a good part of the morning scrolling through her own and Miranda's photos on their phones, looking for the right one of herself to post? One that would show off her tan, her aging face seen from the most flattering angle. One of her laughing with Giorgos, his arm draped around her shoulders, his pretty young wife nowhere in the frame.

Of course she'd particularly wanted Jeff to see that one.

Tay-Sachs. Yes, Valeria explained to Miranda on the slow and airless elevator ride that night, the Morettis were Ashkenazi Jews who'd changed their names and hidden their Jewish identity when they were first in Rome. They'd arrived with the frail, nearly dying Max Klein, a man they'd met in the camps, and nursed him back to health. Later, after he returned to Holland, he bought the hotel and hired the Morettis to manage it. He loved the films of De Sica and Fellini and Visconti, and so he called it the Hotel Cinecittá, and Signore Moretti named the bar the Ristorante Utrecht, in honor of Mr. Klein's beloved home city, which the Morettis had visited once, before their first daughter was born.

When they reached their floor and the elevator's outer gate creaked open, Valeria held the door open only long enough to give each of them a brisk hug and tell them goodnight.

Miranda was crying softly by the time they stepped into their suite and Fran switched on the light. "I can't believe you didn't tell me any of that," she said.

And what could Fran say to that? How could she admit that she she'd forgotten those details about the Moretti family's past—if she'd even known them. And that she'd known nothing about Valeria's child. That, at least, she was sure of.

Fran slept very little that night. She kept thinking about another thing Valeria had told them that evening as she turned off lights—in the office, behind the front desk, above the hotel's entrance and sign—and locked various and sundry doors. Which was that Kostas had used drugs for a very long time. But he'd been clean for a while, briefly, back when he came back to the Hotel Cinecittá to find her and court her and marry her. Until their child died. Then he'd slid away and never returned. Heroin mostly, Valeria said, but other things now too apparently. The worst, the lowest street drugs.

Valeria gave him money, still, when he asked, even though it enraged her sister every time. Though he'd lived in Athens for years he still showed up in Rome from time to time, to ask for more. Every time he asked he promised it would be the last. But she'd stopped believing that long ago, she said, pressing the button for the elevator.

There were things you didn't post, Fran thought now, wide awake at three AM. Often the most important things, the things that had indelibly shaped your life. Your family's secret history. Your marriage to a junkie. Your daughter's slow, sure drift away from you. Your husband's thoughtless and fleeting affair all those years ago. And your chronic thoughts of leaving him.

The death of your only child.

Finally Fran rose from her bed to walk into the next room and stare at her sleeping daughter. Valeria had insisted on giving them the hotel's only suite, though she and Carlotta could have made a good deal of money on that room, surely, during this, the high season for tourists in Rome. For some reason, when Fran thought of that again, she finally began to weep. Only then.

When Miranda slept Fran could still sometimes see, in her face, the child that she'd once been. Now it was hard to make that image of her daughter fit with the long, tanned thigh poking out from under the sheet, the bare arm covering her bare breasts.

And then, from nowhere, an image flashed in Fran's mind, of Valeria as a younger woman. She was seated somewhere, looking as she'd looked as a girl but draped in a flowing black robe. Like the Virgin in a *Pietá*. Holding her dead daughter. Then she saw Kostas, ragged and ghostlike, floating behind his wife and daughter, a figure from an Expressionist painting maybe. Out of sync like that, messing with the composition.

Below her Miranda suddenly stirred, then threw her arm over her head and spoke aloud—a rush and tumble of words, incomprehensible—before she turned on her side and settled. She'd always done that, had talked in her sleep like that since she was tiny, Fran was thinking, and then—oh God—it came to her, and her quiet weeping turned to sobbing, and she left her daughter's room so she wouldn't wake her.

To have not known Miranda at five, at twelve. To not know her *now*.

There were things you didn't post, and also things, like the death of an infant child, that were simply too terrible to ponder. So terrible, and so unfathomable to the mother of two healthy children, that they hadn't even made it onto Fran's list.

Interior layout by Sky Santiago.

The original interior design
for the American Storytellers Series
is by David James.
It is set in Sabon LT Standard
with Nexa Light page headers and chapter titles.

CPSIA information can be obtained
at www.ICGtesting.com
Printed in the USA
BVHW030838070520
579357BV00001B/151